Contents

Colophon

While the title says "autobiographies," these stories are works of fiction. If it sounds real, well, that's what a writer does.

While some of the names and places are real, what happens with them in these stories is not. I have used my official creative license (shown upon request) with people, history, time, space, and action.

A note about the fonts in the printed edition: The body copy is *PMN Caecilia* by Peter Matthias Noordzij https://www.teff-type.com. The cover type and headlines are in the wonderful free *Retro Signature* by Nirmana Visual. https://nirmanavisual.com/

Thanks!

To my friends and family—both biological and logical. You know who you are. I love and am grateful for you! (Especially the playful ones.)

I'd also like to thank the characters who told me their stories. Writing is about getting out of your own way and listening.

Cover and book design by the author.

You can blame him if you think the handwriting font is hard to read but he won't care—it's his book. Play your cards right and you can choose the fonts for your own book, too.

www.WILL-HARRIS.COM

i am art

I live inside any image. Don't just look. *See* me. *Feel* me.

I imbue inanimate materials with my energy —long gone but not forgotten.

Take me home. I will share myself with you. All the good. And the good of the bad.

You can make of me what you will. Cipher. Ghost. Spirit. Or simply shape and color.

I will watch over you—and if you listen I will speak. When I have nothing more to say to you, it is time to give me to someone else so that I might whisper in their ear, tickle their fancy, warm their heart.

I am here. But you must take time to see and feel me. If you do, I am here—*for you.*

Inside the Monkey House

Ah, the thrill of the city. Everyone I knew had traded their young lives for it. The clean air in their lungs replaced with soot. The bird calls with tinnitus. Fresh picked berries with an odd assortment of rubber bits between one's teeth. But the city was where he was, thus it was where I was, too.

But unlike most city boys who are bred into the place, I had begun my young life in the wholesome countryside of N17, a goodly distance from the crowded core as there was no tube at the time and buses were few and far between.

So I made do with the marshes and fishes and farms. I watched the skyline from a distance, heard the occasional aircraft, and endured parental stories on the horror of war and how their suffering had paved the way to my idyllic youth. Good on them.

My mother was a former air warden and seamstress. My bookish father preferred the company of a tome to a Thom, meaning me, so I was stuck between a shrew and a dead place.

Growing up like an animal, you are, father would occasionally hiss between puffs on his pipe. An animal without much guidance from a father too busy collecting rare books and a mother too interested in the lives of others, yet strangely not his.

For many years he assumed he had simply landed in the wrong house. Crawled there by mistake as an infant, taken in, as adults must do when a child appears. Meanwhile, his real parents went off to the jungle somewhere in the dark continent he had read about in one of his father's books.

He was housed and fed, as foreign children were by kind Englishmen and women during the war. But the war had ended years before, so there was always a slight possibility that he was their child by birth. Still, it was something he was loath to consider as he had seen creatures consummate such acts and could not envision those two engaged in such a ritual.

He also often thought of himself in the third person, as he is doing now, as if he watched himself from afar. A character in one of his father's books, one perhaps interesting enough to warrant his father reading about.

Yet it was also an affectation his father might have called ego-maniacal and highly inappropriate if his father had bothered to notice him.

Time passed. Pants grew shorter. Shoes smaller, still, then discarded for bare feet, the soles of which had turned blackish from mucking about by the river.

He was perfectly happy, at least what he thought was happy, except when he was forced to wash up and go to school! Why? He already knew how to read and write. He already knew where the sun rose and set. He already knew which leaves were edible and which would make a person ill. What more did he need to know?

So he would trudge off to school, then be distracted by a lark or a bluebird or a squirrel or a trenchant beetle. And only when the sun was setting, realized he needed to wash up in the river, clothe and shod himself, and slink back to the place where his apparent parents were.

The next day he awoke with the sun, as always, if not a few minutes before, and listened to the surprising quiet. Ah, it must be a Saturday, he thought to himself, without quotation marks, as he felt these should be eliminated in literature, finding them poncy.

Not having to pretend to go to school today, he would have more time to muck about in the muddy Lee. Bliss.

Just then, his mother's broad, red face appeared like an apparition above him on the sofa where he slept.

Get up, ya little animal, she growled, again, without quotation marks.

He rubbed his eyes, this was not the spectre one expected or enjoyed seeing first thing. Normally his mother thing left him alone while she puttered about making tea for herself and father. So why, on a Saturday of all days, was she showing her face to him in such a ghastly display.

Why, he asked himself with alarm, was she wearing a hat?

That could mean only one thing, that they were -going out- he thought, so aghast he felt the need for some kind of punctuation to enliven the statement.

-Going out- was never good. It meant endless trips to the shops, where other mothers would engage in a kind of pack activity over cheese. Presenting themselves in odd ways, using voices that sounded unnatural, and pointing to their children as if possessions they had won at a carnival.

Sally has won a prize! One would say, with a verbal exclamation mark. Sally was always winning this or that. Most often the disdain of other children who disliked her intensely. Sally was a snitch, who, if she saw you walking away from school when you were expected to be walking towards it, would tell an adult who would tell another and soon people were out looking for you which was highly unnecessary and unappreciated.

Having a beetle in my pocket, which I so often did, I placed it gingerly on the pink ruffled back of this monster girl and waited, quite angelically, as it crawled into her curly red hair.

For once I hoped to look as if I was the model boy. Standing straight, hands in pockets, a quick spit on the old hand and brushing through the old hair so as to look as normal as possible... and then...

A shriek that could have awoken the dead, and maybe did, I don't know, I was in a cheese shop, not a cemetery. Then hysterical writhing, some of it on the floor soiling the pink dress, much of it involving tears and a swarm of painted fingernails sorting through said hair to find the bit of nature that had managed to find its way near the girl's empty head.

And all the while I stood, stock still, thinking about how best to adjust my face into an expression of concern. Then I felt a hand brush past my head, as mother pushed my shoulder towards the door, lest other bits or bobs might be finding their way onto my head, as sometimes happened at school.

Poor Sally, I thought, would she ever be the same? I hoped not! I liked question marks? Yes, I did? I did! And exclamation marks, too, which father found frivolous.

Now, once again back into the sunshine, I felt my mother's paw holding me still by the bus stop of all places. The bus! The last time I was on a bus we went to see her mother and father, two sloth-like creatures who smelled of onion and ammonia. We sat in their dark parlor, the draperies shut, and drank oniony tea. There weren't even biscuits!

I was partial to biscuits. Occasionally, when I caught a yellow wren, I would carry him or her to Dr. Martin's house, knowing how Dr. Martin, rare among adults, actually cared for animals, being a veterinarian as such.

Dr. Martin loved birds and had built, all by himself, an enclosure the size of a bus, filled with colorful birds which he fed fruit, better than any I had at home. He would talk to them sweetly, like the babies they seemed to be to him, after his wife, Althea, passed away. Though I once heard mother tell father that Althea had -bolted- again he felt the need to use some sort of punctuation to highlight a word he did not seem to understand, knowing only of bolts that held things together, not tore them apart.

Dr. Martin, always kind to me, would give me tea and biscuits, and 10 shillings, which I would generally spend on more biscuits, consumed in a leisurely fashion whilst lounging by the river, lest anyone else try to eat them.

I might someday want to become a veterinarian myself, I told Dr. Martin, who was always encouraging of such a plan.

I would like to cure sick animals, the way you do, Doctor Sir.

Dr. Martin had, on more than one occasion, suggested I call him Hugh. But having never called an adult by their given name, this felt foreign to me. I preferred to refer to him as Doctor Sir, which seemed to make him smile.

Several afternoons a week, ostensibly after school hours, I would appear at his back door, let myself in, and make myself useful in his cage room where animals recovered. I would feed them, check their dressings, apply unguents as necessary, and sometimes sing songs to them if they seemed amenable.

Dr. Martin said that -music soothed the savage beast- but these cats, dogs, and even the horses or pigs who would stay in the back did not seem like beasts to me, no more than I was a beast myself. They were more humane than the humans I knew. Except for Dr. Martin, who, as far as I could tell, would soon be sainted.

But this afternoon I was standing at a bus stop of all places, my mother's firm hand holding me in place lest I, what, dart in front of an oncoming bus? As if!

The large red vehicle arrived, shining in the sun like a massive ladybug. My mother continued to hold me back, allowing others to trundle on first as she nodded in mock consideration to them.

Once finally planted on an itchy seat, the bus started in motion, something that felt at first like a horse, then unnaturally like somehow swimming along the street. Quite unsettling.

I remembered, once, when I was younger and we were headed to mother's parents, I felt the need to vomit, which, unfortunately, landed on her shiny new shoes. I thought I would never hear the end of that!

And even now, she is sitting sideways, her feet protruding into the aisle, far from any possible contamination.

But I am no longer a child! I am 12 years old. Or so she told me, then and there, saying, -you are no longer a child, Thomas, you are 12 years old. Happy Birthday-

What? I was quite taken aback by this statement, having imagined that a dozen years old would feel different than it currently felt. But, not keeping track of such things, I could only defer to her on this and imagine that she was being forthright in her assumption.

So I was now a man, or close to it. Despite not having seen or felt any kind of beard growing anywhere on my person.

I had read father's biology books, I had seen other boys get older, so I knew such things happened and checked, every day, to see if they were happening to me, and since they were not, I was unaware how much time had passed.

-I have a birthday surprise for you!- mother said in a delighted tone I could only surmise was designed to impress those around us. I was so surprised by the tone I thought it must be the surprise.

But no, there was more.

-I am taking you to the zoo!" she said, loud enough for all around to hear. I was so shocked that I envisioned a closing quotation mark as she ended her statement.

I had never been to the zoo. I had heard about it, of course, on rainy days when going to class seemed preferable to shivering in a stream. Other children talked about their -trip- and described animals I already knew in great detail from books. At first I thought they must be prevaricating, as live African animals could not possibly feel at home in this cold clime.

But then I went to the Z section of father's library and read about these zoo places and thought it would be wonderful to go and asked my mother, as asking my father anything was an exercise in futility.

Mother said -as if we are made out of money Thomas- a statement wholly unworthy of quotation marks or even commas.

But what care I for zoos when I have wild animals and Dr. Martin's ever changing menagerie?

We got off the 76 bus and onto one marked 11. It was stifling in the hot sun and I longed to open the window the way other children had. But I knew what mother would say about her hair. Thomas, do you really want your mother to look like a pagan?

Mother felt unkempt hair gave one the look of a pagan, quite obviously, though just as obviously from my reading one could not distinguish a person's beliefs by their hairstyles, except perhaps for monks.

So I sat in the sun and the heat and I hoped this would not lead to any kind of involuntary purging, even though her feet were still carefully placed as far from my mouth as one could place them and still sit on the same seat.

I watched the world fly by. So many unnecessary things. Shops and cars and overcoats. One only needed animals, rivers and books, really, if one considered it, but other people apparently did not.

I did enjoy seeing the dogs, sadly on leashes, and birds, free in the trees. I almost pushed mother aside and decanted the bus to climb a tree full of redwing blackbirds, but she pushed back, harder.

Finally the bus stopped in front of a set of large iron gates. On the top was a lion, covered in gold! Mother grasped my damp hand. It was not my fault it was damp, even though she looked at me as if it was. She slid her hand out of mine, wiped it on the leg of my short pants, then pushed me from behind and led me off the bus.

"ROYAL LONDON ZOO" was written out in iron below the lion. Perhaps it was because these animals were royal that they could live outside their normal habitat, the way the queen lived outside a normal human habitat and survived in the ghastly palace I'd seen in books.

I already liked the smell of the place. Dung and straw and candy floss. Mother immediately sat herself on a bench and said, -go and be back in an hour.-

I ran. Not even wondering how I would know what an hour was, and not caring even after hearing the church bell ring.

I ran so as not to miss anything. Not the daring pink flamingos standing in water while balanced on one leg. Not the tortoise whose sign claimed he was 127 years old. Not the elephants who one was allowed to touch. They felt like nothing else I had ever felt, except maybe for mother's father with his rough skin and hard hair.

Oh, the glory of the place! I was at once enthralled to be here and angry it took a full dozen years to get here. Knowing it was within the purview of just two buses I might use future shillings from Dr. Martin to find my own way here in future!

And now I was standing in the monkey house. Nothing but a few iron bars between me and black furry boys, or so they seemed to me. They sat on their ample behinds, their delicate fingers wrapped around the iron.

I had only seen animals in cages at Dr. Martin's and then they were in recovery, as he called it, so it was fine. But suddenly, I saw these boys, perhaps my age, as prisoners.

I reached out to touch one of their hands, not paws, but actual hands, but it was too far away. One reached his furry hand towards me and our fingers almost touched.

Then I looked into his watery brown eyes and saw he was looking straight into mine. Dogs and cats had looked at me, horses, pigs and even goats, but this was different. This boy was looking right at me, young man to young man.

I longed to sit with him, naked as he was, feeling his shiny fur and picking nits off each other. How lovely.

How sad that he was a prisoner in this cage.

I felt like a prisoner in my home and school, too, but at least I was free to roam about when adults weren't paying attention, which was much of the time.

So I wondered if any adults were paying attention here. There was one, wearing a military looking khaki suit with many shiny buttons and a large ring of keys dangling from his belt.

He was tipping his hat to a pretty-ish young woman in a blue polka dot dress then chatting her up.

He did not display much interest in the captivating creatures in the cage, or the children throwing candy cones at them. Or even the bright ape who could catch the cones, mid-air, with one hand, while the other was hurling his own feces back at the screaming kiddies, sending them scurrying.

-smells like shit in here- I said, sidling up to the polka dot girl, too close, hoping to encourage her to go outside with her erstwhile beau.

She seemed to smell the place for the first time, held her nose, as he held the door and followed her out, not even noticing as I slipped the ring of keys from his belt.

I went immediately to the heavy steel door and quickly tried every key until one opened, then I slipped inside. But I was not inside the cage, as I had thought, no, I was inside a hallway, lined with flowered wallpaper and photos of a family of humans, first a couple, then with a baby, two small children, and two small children and two apes, all sitting on their lap.

There was another door at the end of the hallway, and it was ajar, so I let myself in only to find a Victorian sitting room, worse for wear, dimly lit with gas light.

The floor was littered with children's toys, some chewed beyond recognition. The shelves were lined with leather-bound books, possibly well read, certainly well chewed. The far wall was odd, with a row of iron bars in front of dark wood paneling.

Another door, this one closed. I had forgotten the keys on the sofa, so I retrieved them and started to try them in the lock when I heard a voice on the other side.

-Walter?- the voice said, and the door was opened by a mature woman with white hair, her thin hand rising to her mouth in surprise.

-You are not Walter, young man. How did you find your way in?- she asked, not unkindly.

-I wanted to meet the monkeys- I said, rather dumbly, but it seemed to be a good answer as she smiled, opened the door and said -then you have come to the right place, my boy!- with an exclamation mark of joy in her voice.

Inside the door was another room like something from a museum. This one a kitchen, with a round wooden table and eight chairs, in which were sitting 12 small apes, eating off blue and white metal plates with silver cutlery. They all turned, briefly, and looked at me, then went back to their meal.

-Sorry they aren't more sociable, my dear, it's lunchtime you see- and I did see. There were piles of crustless sandwiches and towers of colorful little cakes.

The apes ate in a more orderly way than my mates, and chattered with each other in a language that felt familiar.

-Help yourself to a sandwich, my boy- the nice lady suggested. One of the apes looked at me and patted the chair next to him. The woman said, "Thank you, Angus," and I joined him, selecting a sandwich that looked like cucumber because whenever possible, I preferred not to eat animals.

The ape was as soft as I thought he might be, though smelled quite a bit more. But not in a bad way, no, more like a hot horse does, in that lovely musky way. I felt him lean into me and I leaned back, feeling his warmth.

He took his sandwich, filled with a pinkish cream I took to be salmon, and pressed it to my lips. I took a bite. Salmon. I didn't mind eating fish. I smiled and nodded. Then I took my sandwich and pressed it against his mouth and he took a bite and nodded back.

And there we sat for I don't know how long as I'd long since stopped listening for church bells. Happily lunching with a lad who at last felt my equal.

After nothing was left on the table (he'd taken the last cake, given me a bite, then finished it), he took my hand in his. And what a lovely hand. Warm and soft and smooth on one side, and warm and softly furry on the other.

He led me out into a tall space with rocks and tree trunks where the others were happily playing and grooming each other. He reached into my hair, rooted around, and pulled out a bug which he promptly ate. It seemed the most natural thing in the world. So I proceeded to do the same for him. It was not the first time I had eaten a bug, but it was the first time I had eaten one off a chum.

I felt, quite deeply, that Angus was the kindest creature I had ever met. And more than that, I felt like I was finally home. Angus introduced me to his friends, all of whom rooted through my hair, mostly coming away empty handed.

And, by turn, they lightly touched my face with their warm, soft hands, and I touched their faces back.

The old woman called, "Angus" in such a sweet way it was worthy of quote marks. He took my hand and we went to her, back into the kitchen.

"Angus has always been special, he does tea with us." At the table were sitting an old man, and two human children about my age. "This is my husband, Walter. We have lived here and taken care of the monkey cage since before the war. And this is our granddaughter, Alice, and grandson, Luke."

Angus gently pushed my back so I would step up to them and shake hands. Walter ruffled through my hair, much as the apes did and looked slightly disappointing not finding anything in it.

"Sit here," Luke said, patting the chair next to him in much the same way that Angus had. I sat, and Angus sat on my lap.

"My, he's taken a shine to the new boy, hasn't he, Mary?" Walter said as Mary carried a tray of sandwiches exactly like the ones I'd just had.

Luke smiled at me and said, "That's because the boy's part ape, like us, gramps!" and they all chortled. I laughed, too, but then stopped, because what he said was true. I had read Darwin, I was part ape, but I also knew he meant it in a different sort of way, a way of welcoming.

Angus climbed onto the table, picked up the teapot and did the honors of filling our cups and placing sandwiches on our plates.

There was so much love here. Love like I had never felt except in Dr. Martin's recovery room. Love and care and genuine delight at being in each others' company.

I was so happy I began to cry and Angus wiped my tear with his soft finger, then stuck it in his mouth.

Luke put his hand on my shoulder and just kept it there. Nobody besides Dr. Martin and Angus had ever done that.

"I'm sorry, I am being ridiculous," I said, saying the same thing I'd heard my father say once when I found him crying over a book.

"Not at all," Luke said, kindly, "Angus is particularly lovely."

And he was! Just hearing Luke say that made me laugh. I still felt ridiculous, laughing and crying at the same time and needing desperately to blow my nose. But I knew I was amongst friends here.

Angus pressed a tea cake to my lips and I took a bite, then he took a bite, then he proceeded to feed the last bit to Luke.

"I'm so glad you found your way here," said Alice, clearly the nicest girl I had ever met, even if she was reading a book at the same time. "Luke was getting lonely," she said, teasingly.

"I was not, I'm never lonely with Angus here!" he said, pulling Angus close.

But Angus shook his head, "No!" emphatically, quote marks and all. I now felt the overwhelming urge to root through Luke's yellow hair, which made him smile.

"Seems like you've found a human mate at last," Walter said, one hand holding his teacup, the other gently rooting through his wife's white hair.

Oh, how I wished that time would stop here and now. How I wished it might be my 12th birthday forever and ever and that I might never have to go home.

The plan came instantly to my mind, that I would speak with Dr. Martin and tell him of my desire to work with animals, which he already knew, but now to work on the monkey house. And he, a licensed man of animals, would speak to the licensed animal man here and come to an agreement that this is where I should live and work. Yes, that is how it would happen, I was sure of it.

This plan only gained resilience in my mind as I helped Luke muck out the straw bedding in the back, hose it down, then lay fresh straw beds... It became even stronger as we changed Angus' sheets in the room with three beds, one for Alice, one for Luke and one for Angus who did not wet his bed, but did shed.

I looked around the room, seeing a place for another bed and planning my future here.

Then Luke and Angus and I went to the play area and watched the sun set through the bars, a lovely sight, so peaceful until shattered by a scream, "THERE HE IS! STOLEN BY BEASTS!"

And there she was, my beastly mother, pointing at me from the other side of the bars. "What is wrong with you people? He could be killed, get him out of there immediately!"

And so the men came.

Angus took my hand and pulled me up the trees to the top of the enclosure as I extended my hand for Luke to follow. The policemen were unable to climb the slippery trees and so they stood, below, shaking their sticks.

Angus looked at them, then at me, then at a pile of bananas up on the ledge. I knew we could be here a long time.

"You dunces!" my mother beast shrieked, as she stormed into the cage, While the young apes had ignored the men, they scattered and hid at my mother's intrusion. The air was charged with tension and fear. I smelled shit and wondered if it was mine.

"You get down here this very instant!" she commanded in her booming air warden voice. And I, as I had always done, began to comply, stopped only by Luke's firm grip on my wrist. He shook his head. So did Angus.

It was a standoff. I knew she would want to sit down soon enough and might then forget about me, coming home by herself, father not even noticing.

The white haired lady appeared and said to my beet red mother, "Care for a cuppa?" at which my mother began to fade, and, seeing a way out, answered, "Bless you, my dear" and started towards the door.

But her hasty retreat was not to be, for at just that moment I saw Angus's nostrils flare, and he leapt down the tree and straight at my mother!

And for the first time, I felt a protective instinct for this creature, this woman. I slid down the tree and jumped between Angus and her and held her tight. And for the first time, I felt her shaking with fear, holding me more tightly than she ever had before.

It was very quiet, even as Angus climbed up my back and sat on my shoulder, running his hand through mother's hair. She put her head on my shoulder, thinking the hand was mine, though I would never have thought to touch her that way.

Then I heard a sound I did not know existed —I heard her crying.

"Oh, if only your mother was here," she said.

"Well, I'll be a monkey's uncle," I thought. Everything made sense. And suddenly this beast became a person, if not a mother.

I felt my shirt grow wet with her tears as I watched Angus stroke her head. He'd managed to pull out something I never could.

Cadaver Flower

Weeping willows, always my favorite. So beautiful yet sad. Like me.

Momma always said a young lady looks much prettier when she's a little bit unhappy. Young ladies who smile are trollops.

She need not have worried—I rarely smiled. Nor was there so much as a dollop of trollop in me.

No, I considered myself an exotic blossom, like the Century Flower I read about once in the library. It only bloomed once every hundred years.

I looked in the glass, inspecting my face for any hint of a smile. No. My skin was white as cream and soft as velvet. Or so the boys who courted me would say. I knew they wanted to lap up that cream like a kitten. But the only way they could touch me was with their eyes, and that I think was the secret. For the other girls who would appear rumpled from the veranda, their hair mussed, those girls did not have the longest line of beaus waiting to dance with them, no sir.

Why? Because boys did not have to wait for those girls. But they would have to wait for me.

Maybe 100 years they would have to wait.

When a boy was serious, I would say to him, "Will you wait for me?" and he would nod, like a puppy dog, and say, "Oh yes, Magnolia, yes."

"Would you wait a hundred years?" I'd ask. They'd look confused, like how could they possibly do that, but still they'd say, "Oh yes, Magnolia, yes."

Their desperate faces made me happy for one brief moment. I would sometimes look back on their pathetic entreats and think, "Oh, Magnolia, you do know what happiness is, you felt it for that one little smidgen of time."

I considered myself lucky because I was not convinced anyone else had actually ever felt it. Momma said "Just because those idiots are running around grinning does not mean they is happy."

Happiness felt like the furthest thing, that winter's day, when I was staring out the window at the wet weeping willows. Lovely, lugubrious trees, made even more melancholy by the tears from heaven.

Momma came in, she said, "Magnolia we must have a dress made for you as the Winter Ball is coming."

I did not answer her. I just kept looking at those mournful trees in the rain.

She said, "Magnolia! I am speaking to you, your mother is speaking to you. I deserve the honor of an answer!"

So I tore my eyes away from those glistening green leaves and I said to her, "I know what I want, Momma, I want a weeping willow dress."

Momma just shook her head and made that clicking noise with her mouth the way she so often did.

"Oh you crazy girl! Your Poppa is plum crazy, you get it from him."

I said, "No, Momma, I know what I want. I want spring leaf green lace, touched with crystals, like raindrops."

"Magnolia! Nobody wears spring green to a winter dance! It can be dark green if you insist but it must be paired with red, you know very well you can't parade around in spring green like some trollop!"

There she was again with her trollop, as if by not being dressed as a Christmas tree I might suddenly lose my morals and find myself on my back in the bushes with my feet in the air like Cornelia.

Cornelia once told me about her escapades and I was simply mortified. It was bad enough when a boy touched my hand with his warm sticky fingers, I did not want any other part of him coming in contact with me!

Maybe, someday, after my wedding vows, I might possibly allow a man to kiss me—but what Cornelia described was nothing short of a horror story, like the boogie man Momma would threaten me with when I was bad.

I thought Cornelia must be making it up—she spouted quite a load of nonsense. I could not, for the life of me, imagine my Momma doing anything as heinous as that, and my father was certainly too much of a gentleman.

Besides, how could civilized people ever look at each other after such a thing? No, it had to be a product of her fevered imagination!

"MAGNOLIA!" Momma was practically shouting now. She had this way about her of talking very loud whereas I rarely spoke above a whisper.

One time I almost said to her, I said, "Momma, only trollops speak so loudly," but I knew she would have slapped my face and I didn't want any marks on my perfect cheeks, so I held my tongue.

I apologized to Momma for being off in my own little world—but I stood firm. I would have that weeping willow dress.

Momma kept tittering on about how she could "add some red feathers or red shoes or something..." as if I wanted to look like all the rest of those chicken-livered girls, thinking that a touch of red would make me more appealing to the menfolk.

The next day we went to see Miss Vernetta, our dressmaker. Normally, we would have brought our own fabric purchased in New Orleans, or anyplace more cosmopolitan than Charlotte. But I was standing firm on my idea of green lace, and Momma finally gave in knowing there was nothing she could do about "her crazy girl!" We knew Miss Vernetta would have some lace she could dye.

Miss Vernetta was a funny old thing, shaped like a thimble herself. Large bosom always tightly constricted in her cotton dresses, the hips of a mule, pudgy little hands that somehow managed to create the finest tiny stitches as if a fairy had made them.

She did have lace. She brought it out with an apology, saying, "I'm sorry, Magnolia, this is all I have and nobody wants it."

Momma gasped in horror when she saw it. I gasped, too—it was perfect!

Momma said, "You're right, Vernetta, nobody in their right mind would have that."

I said, "I will have it, momma."

It was as if her eyes might have rolled right out of her head. She pulled me aside by the arm, nearly giving me a mark and said, "Magnolia Trepidation Wallace, why on earth would you want anything as hideous as that, I put my foot down, I refuse!"

This is when my constant state of sadness was at its most useful and perhaps appealing.

I let my sorrow rise to the surface and a single tear dripped daintily from my right eye. I sniffed and dabbed at it with my hankie, as if trying to hide it from her but that was the furthest thing from the truth.

I whispered, "All right, Momma. If you want to make me the unhappiest girl in all of Charlotte, then fine, I shall bow to your wishes and I shall not go to the dance."

It was all I could do to keep from saying, "What do you know of fashion, Mother? All of Charlotte is still gossiping about your last gown!" I had, in fact, heard others talking about her ox-blood dress with too many layers of flounces.

I remember her coming back from Vernetta's with it and saying, "It positively lights up my face!" and I thought, "It positively lights up a room like some kind of terrible explosion from the war!"

But she would not be deterred and she flounced with her flounces into that ball as if she was 17 again. I was positively mortified, and she was smiling—like a trollop!

When she got home, she gushed, "Magnolia, I do believe that was the best ball I have ever attended, I felt like a girl again! And I do believe your father was smitten!"

I do believe she was right about father, who was notoriously colorblind, and therefore could find her appealing. I was happy for them.

Ah—another moment of happiness. I must write it down in my little book. I had started making notes of such moments.

Now, of course, back to my tears, Momma had become slightly immune to them, but not Miss Vernetta. I've no doubt she had seen this act on numerous occasions from countless young ladies. Wanting to curry their favor and continue to make their gowns, she would cleverly take their side, but so gently that their mothers might think she was actually taking theirs.

Vernetta said, "Charlaine, I could, in fact, make this quite new, like a rotogravure I saw in a magazine from Paris, France."

While I imagine she was simply trying to get rid of a run of lace she had not been able to pawn off on anyone since the reconstruction, I added, though a sniffle, "You know, Momma, styles have changed since you were a girl," which I said in such a nice way she could not possibly take offense.

I saw her eyes looking around, as if to imagine her friends at the ball, watching me enter, trying to predict how mortified she might be by me.

I'd heard stories about how she'd been a strong-willed young woman herself. She must have understood, because with the tiniest of nods she relented.

And so, it came to pass. After numerous drawings I tore gently out of my little book, myriad fittings and many conspiratorial whispers between Vernetta and myself, I was to be a "Winter Weeping Willow."

Vernetta, who fancied herself as an artist, said she did believe she had never made as lovely a gown. I had to agree with her.

The rose of my skin was set off by the leafy green lace, which by itself might have been rather hideous. But when layered in such a manner, like leaves, and touched with dew-drop crystals, it was nothing less than a vision!

And now it was Vernetta's turn to shed a tear, only this one I believed sincere.

When she said to me, "It hardly seems fair for me to take your father's money when I have had the joy of creating this," I once again held my sometimes sharp tongue and avoided saying, "Then maybe you should not!"

But how could I deny her due, when she had created what I could only think of as a bespoke portrait of myself.

When Momma saw it, her eyes got wide and she nodded her head and smiled and said, "Magnolia, you do have a way with you!"

Then she fussed around Vernetta's looking for red accessories, to which I said, "Momma, I have already decided on my jewels. I wish to wear your diamond drop earrings, if you would be so kind."

Now, I knew that these earrings were Momma's prize possessions. She had told me I might, just might, wear them at my wedding.

But I was starting to feel like my hundred years was coming due, and that in this dress, I might finally bloom.

Then I felt my face take on the strangest expression, as if a smile was growing beneath my skin.

I do believe Momma saw it, too as she nodded again, and said, "Yes, Magnolia, my dear, that would be perfection."

Somehow everything felt too wonderful. There were so many notations in my book of moments of happiness sometimes stretching out to entire minutes of happiness. It was shocking.

As I started to feel these twinges of happiness more often, I also started to feel an undercurrent of dread, as if it was not natural for one to feel so much joy.

When I would feel that dread I would simply go to the wardrobe, open it and gaze upon my weeping willow dress, touching it lightly with my fingertips.

Then I would feel that smile creeping up on me again. A feeling I was becoming so reliant on, like Poppa and his medicinal morphine.

As the days inched closer to the ball, arrangements were made. The carriage was polished, footmen ready. Samantha was called to do my hair.

But oddly, I began to feel that instead of going to a ball I was going to a funeral.

It made no sense to me and I thought I must be losing my mind. It must have been the happiness that done it!

Too much happiness is not normal, not right, not good for one's constitution.

And yet, there I was, happy and horrified at the same moment.

It was then I decided I must go back to the library and read more about this flower that bloomed every hundred years to find out what it might feel like when I finally blossomed.

I re-read the familiar page, but now I noticed that the thin vellum pages had been stuck together and I had missed the second page entirely!

After carefully separating the pages, I read, in horror, how the Century Flower was also called the "Cadaver Flower," because of its nauseating stench!

I did not know what to do. I came home and told mother I could not go to the Ball.

Now she actually did put her tiny little foot down and she said, "Magnolia, it is one thing to be crazy and it is another thing to be outright cuckoo bird. I put up with your craziness, but I will not, I repeat, I will not have insanity in my family again! I refuse to let you turn out like Mad Aunt Alice in Shreveport who is not allowed out of the attic!"

This time there was no dissuading her. I thought about my alternatives. Maybe I would throw myself out of the carriage on the way, but I couldn't bear to soil the gown.

Maybe I would be forced to swallow some lye and be violently ill...

I simply could not go tonight! I could not be revealed as a Cadaver flower!

With every tick of the clock, and every shadow that grew, my dread grew with it. I felt my stomach turn even without lye and I refused all food.

Mother thought nothing of it because she often would starve herself before a dance so that she might look more svelte.

But I felt like Aunt Alice. I wished that somebody would lock me in the attic and not let me out!

If Momma only knew the dread and terror that would be raining down upon our family... She would gladly lock me up herself.

So I finally mustered up the courage to say to her, "Momma! I am going to stink tonight!"

That made her laugh. "Magnolia, you are many things, but a stinker you are most certainly not." She leaned in and I felt her nose against my neck. She inhaled. I had not yet applied any scent and she still said, "My darling girl, you are sweet."

But then, I had not yet bloomed.

I was helped into the dress, and I needed but look at myself in the mirror to feel that idiot smile growing inside me.

No—this dress would not look right with a smile, not right at all. But with my innate air of sadness, it did look most wonderful.

I focused on that—and feeling the tendrils of lace between my fingertips. Noticing the sparkle of crystal from the corner of my eye.

I steeled myself, "This is what you shall do, Magnolia, you will sparkle, like a weeping willow in the rain. No one need know you are blossoming. They may look no deeper than the dress."

So I put on my moss green velvet cape. I stepped in the carriage. I listened to the horse's hooves. I smelled the crisp winter air. I saw the lights of the town hall as we drew near.

I felt at once, like a bride, and a corpse.

The marshal took my hand and led me off the carriage and walked with me, on his arm, into the ballroom, where I was announced.

"Miss Magnolia Trepidation Wallace."

All eyes were upon me. All voices were hushed. Smiles faded into as if stunned.

In that silence—I felt an unnatural wave of joy upon me, as if I was, at last, showing the world my true colors. As if, for the first time ever, they were seeing the real Magnolia Trepidation Wallace—And the sight of me was so rare that they simply did not know what to do.

Whether they thought I had a stench like a corpse flower, or saw my insane inner glow of joy shining through the weeping willow, I did no longer care.

As I walked down the stairs, they parted, as if for a queen in her honor.

And I felt myself bloom.

Quadtanium

I won't even buy it if it's not Quadtanium. QVC has the best and I see it on TV then it arrives in two days because I'm a Quad Qlub founding member.

The Quadtanium collection is the best. The very, very, very, very best. It's quad or it's four times better. They're not old-fashioned diamonds—no, they're better—with more sparkle because of the patented Quadtanium cut. It's what the Q in QVC really stands for, at least to my mind.

They all think I'm rich, when I show up at church. 'Cause I look rich. And I should, because I have what I once heard Pastor Nelson saying was "ex-quizite taste."

I'll show up on Sunday with a big red straw hat covered in red glittered berries and the next week, I'll see three other ladies in big straw hats with glitter berries. Oh, they think they're fooling people 'cause their berries is blue or purple or yellow (I'm looking at you, Tonya, who's ever heard of a yellow berry?).

None of my three husbands have had much bank, but they all had insurance, even if I bought it myself.

And no, I didn't knock them off, I'm a religious woman and Jesus wouldn't cotton to that at all, no, no, no. I even cut down on the salt for Roderick when the doctor said he had high blood pressure. I saw him sneakin' those chips, though, and I wasn't gonna take away his little bit of happiness, cause that's all he had left near the end.

I also have my check every month but that goes to expenses, I pay my bills, girlfriend. Don't look at me and think just because I've got my Quadtanium Dangle Pearlescent

Ex'pressions Spanish-Style Hooplet Earrings that I'm not paying my taxes or insurance. Hells to the no.

Oh, pardon me, Jesus. I know there's nothing all that wrong about saying "Hell" it's not like using the Lord's name in vain but I still try to avoid it, especially when I have clients around.

And I talk about insurance because I know how important it is—I work for an insurance agent, Fred Newman, and I do all the paperwork. And when people call I check their files and tell them if they need more or how to keep it up to date.

You cannot have too much insurance. I even have a rider on my homeowner's for the Quadtanium, because fine jewelry and such is only covered up to $500 and I'm sure I have a lot more than though it changes regularly. But I have a $5,000 rider so if I get jacked or there's a fire or anything I get enough money to replace the treasures I have lost.

And, see, the Quadtanium isn't just beautiful and classy and elegant, like Missy Elliot would wear, even though it is all those things and more. It's spiritual y'all.

Sometimes in church the sun will come in and hit me and I see all them sparkles on the altar and it's like God himself is up there, which of course he is—as if revealed by the sun and my Quadtanium to make it obvious even to non-believers.

That's why I sit in the front row. Pastor Nelson has a spot reserved for me—and it moves according to the seasons so that light always hits me, hopefully at the right point in his sermon, so the church is alive with God's rainbows.

I seen grown men start to cry and speak in tongues and fall down with the shakes of Christ, right there, when they see them sparkles.

So when people say, "How can you afford all that bling, Bessie?" I just look at them, real serious, because I am serious about it, and I say, "How can I not afford to when it brings the light of God to our congregation?"

I called up QVC once and told them that. When they have the Quadtanium on, they ask people who already bought it to call and tell the people who are waiting to buy that they need the big Q.

And that real pretty Kathy Kornbloom, she always wearings the most colorful jackets so you can see how the Quadtanium looks against almost any color, last time it was plum—oh my heavens, I bought that Joan Rivers Plum Soft Shouldered Sueded Microfiber Blazer so fast it would make your head swim, cause they sell out of the fuller sizes you know.

So Kathy asked people to call and I called, it was toll-free, and I said what I'd been practicing to say, I said, "When I wear my Quadtanium to church and the light hits it just right, it can make a believer out of anybody!" And they all looked like I'd revealed a secret of Quadtanium that even they had never known, and they were nodding and looking like they'd seen the light, too.

Right there, on national TV, I did my testifying and I brightened the lives of millions of Christians from coast to coast.

That's also when I bought Liza Minnelli's Venus on the Half Shell Quadtanium Pavé Clam Brooch with genuine Pearlesque. It's set in Quadtanium cut so that it looks like it's just solid pa-vay, that's how you pronounce it. I told Liza she's such an inspiration to me, and you know what? She said I'm an inspiration to her, too! I got a recording of her talking to me on my VHS for the grand kids. It's called "provenance," like the place in France.

The nice thing about being in the insurance office is that people come in to buy life or auto and a lot of them come out wearing a nice piece of Quadtanium I sold them. I like to change it up. Like, this clam pin—I'll wear it a few times, then it'll go in the third drawer on the left, the one with the lock, of course, and then when a nice couple comes in and they just bought a new house, even when you're trying to save money you gotta celebrate the important milestones of your life, that's what Fred tells them and I tell them that, too.

And a nice old lady who came in last week looking all sad because her car had been totaled. She walked out looking like a queen, with my old Madeleine Albright United Nations Dove of Peace brooch with Rubyama eyes, a pair of Missy E sunglasses with Diamonique encrusted temples (I love me some Missy but Diamonique is no Quadtanium), and a Queen Latifa Colors of the Amazon Cockatiel Cocktail Ring.

She left the office grinning from ear to ear. When the sun hit her, I saw God sparkles all over the roll down shade. And I smiled, too, because in my own little way, I was doing God's work.

Kiss of Death

S ome people say I'm a killer. Truth is, I'm a life-bringer. Old things have to die so new things have room to be born. It's as simple as that. Getting rid of that stench of decay, bringing in that fresh scent of green. Know what I mean?

My job's an important part of the ecosystem —nothing can live forever. That's just how the world is made.

It's not like I'm making the decisions on what lives and what dies. No, I leave that to higher powers. Powers that have, let's say, a bigger view.

I have one job and I'm going to do it. I don't have to think about the repercussions because you know what? I believe in Karma. I believe in reincarnation. Everything's going to come back in new forms and that's what the world needs—new growth.

As for Karma and me being the kiss of death? Well like I say, I call it the kiss of life.

So, I'm on Fairfax Ave. Very, very trendy street. These young kids, thinking they're going to live forever. I hate to be the one to burst their bubble, but hey, this is life. I don't make up the rules.

Today I'm going into a place called "Wet Dogs." I don't know what kind of name that is, or why someone wants to wear clothing

that supposedly has been on a damp doggie...
Again, not my place to question these things.

My first step is to start touching the
merchandise. Yeah, I'm getting some dirty
looks—like I'm not supposed to be here. But I
am supposed to be here, so what they want
doesn't matter. There's a bigger picture to
attend to.

I'm gonna spend more time here. My
schedule's pretty open for today. And, Hey,
this is part of the work, right?

I'm picking up a Hoodie. It's got some
squiggly lines on. It looks like a cat giving me
the finger. So I calls the sales guy over. He's a
child with a scrawny beard, not like my big
bushy white beard. I've earned this beard.

I say, "I wanna try this on." And you could
just sense something's not right, 'cause he's
given me this look like, just kinda terrified.
Terrified.

Now I'm not a scary dude. If I had to describe
myself, I would say I look like, like Santa
Claus' younger, thinner nephew. Okay?

I'm not an old guy. But when I was his age, which I don't know, what is he, 12? 20? I thought 30 was old. So yeah, 70. That probably seems old to him, but I know that I've got a long time to go, a good long run yet and I got wisdom on my side, right?

So I say, yeah, "I want to try this in an extra large." He just stares at me again. I have to say, "What? You don't want to sell stuff?"

He wakes up and nods and is like, "Oh yes sir!" I think it's hilarious when kids call me sir.

So he goes to the back and he comes out and he goes, "I'm not sure we have your size."

I say, "Why don't you look a little harder, young man? If you don't have it in this style I'll try on any style."

I see his shoulders slump and his head go down as he slinks back into the back. Poor thing. He senses this is the beginning of the end.

He comes out of dragging this tee shirt that's got what looks like whales on skateboards and I'm like, "Ah, that's very pretty, very pretty. I like the tie dyed blue too. That's gonna look good on me." He looked worse and worse.

I'm not here to hurt the guy. You know what? This is not his shop. He's just an employee. He's going to be fine—land on his feet working in a juice bar, coffee shop, or OnlyFans.

I took off my shirt right there. I don't have any issues with my body. I did when I was younger, but you get over that as you get older. I looked at the young'uns shocked by my hairy chest and I smiled. I put on the whale shirt and, hmm, it's a little bit tight. But you know what, I always liked whales.

I stood in front of the mirror and raised my voice a little. "Hey guys, can you come over here and tell me what you think of this?" The young, hip customers in the store are looking at me like, "You shouldn't be in here, man.

You're too old. You're too ugly," But that's all part of my job? It's all part of the job.

I don't take it personally because their idea of old and ugly are not my idea of old and ugly. I felt ugly when I was young. Now I think I'm sexy.

So they're looking at me and nobody says anything and I'm like, "You think it's a little bit too tight?" And this—I guess it was a girl— pipes up and goes, "Uh, it depends on how you like to wear it."

And at that point I pull up a little extra chest hair around my neck and let it let my stomach out. I say, "Yeah, that's a nice look. You're right. I want to wear it this way. I'm going to take this."

Then I pulled a Hoodie over it and I put on a hat and pretty soon from head to toe I've got their Wet Dogs logo all over me. And I'm like, "yeah man, this is the shit."

I watch the young people leaving the store already cause look, if grandpa's wearing this, it can't be cool anymore.

And that my friend is the *kiss of death*. So I buy all the pieces with the company credit card and I stand outside the door. What's the bouncer gonna say to me? "No old dude, you can't stand here. I've just dropped $642 on a generic hat, ill-fitting tee shirt, hideous hoodie and infantile plastic sandals." I'm a customer, man!

Now my job is just to stand there all day and let everyone see how uncool this brand has become if old fat guys are wearing it.

It won't take long now for the store to close. My boss, the landlord, will jack up the rent and a new, hipper brand will take its place.

It's the circle of life, baby!

The Empress's New Clothes

I've always been at the cutting edge of couture. But I had never felt so free. It fit like a dream, literally like a dream. Like the kind of dream where you're walking around naked, only without so much as a hint of embarrassment, because I knew K-karl had me c-covered. He thought of everything.

This would not be the first time I made history. 50 years ago I was known as Tada Yaguichi's muse as he made his steady march away from constructivism to what he called "Organic Shroudery." Initially outre, once he got there I considered it passé.

That's when I met K-karl, as a young fashion student in Liberia, at that time the fashion capital of the world before that honor moved on to Albuquerque.

Now, a half century later, my collection of K-karl was the most extensive anywhere, even including his own archives, most of which I had purchased. And I continued to be his muse and number one patron.

I would blink funds into K-karl's account, even before he had agreed to sell me the newest numbers from his latest show, knowing he would eventually relent with his trademark giggle and cough.

So when I heard the rumor, I was undeterred —I would be the first.

Yet despite my standing, K-karl's office was unusually c-coy, at first denying the existence of an experimental project, then his android assistant, Mark-IV simply said "no comment at this time, madame," signing off with his usual, "Kisses!"

But Harold, being a master of the market, was privy to news before it happened. So he blinked me a small item about K-karl having been seen at CERN, with an analyst's note saying "It could be related to "The Fog'"

A quick temporal tap teleconnected me to Mark-IV, for no one ever spoke directly to K-karl, due to his well-documented fear of other people's breath. This time, I mentioned "The Fog," and noticed a nano-pause in Mark-IV's otherwise beautiful Egyptian by way of an Argentinian accent.

He started to say, "We have no comment, my love," and then whispered, furtively, "You'll be the first to know, babycakes."

A frisson of delight. I was in.

What I didn't know was whether my arch fashion rival, Lady Helena Hattersley had also been able to glean this information through her husband, Gustav, as he owned large swaths of bandwidth clouds over nine continents. To the casual observer it would seem likely that she had.

But rumors in my own extensive circles were that she and her husband had not seen each other, much less teleconnected for three years, and it would have been just like Gustav to withhold that information out of spite.

Charming.

The next week, I thought nothing when I saw the automatic withdrawal from K-karl's office for 250MT, less than the amount I normally spent a week. Perhaps a previously refused item was now on its way. He could never say "no" for long.

But by the end of the day there were four such withdrawals, and even Harold, normally immune to any and all debits on my account, tapped me as his financial system had raised a red flag (one I had K-karl design!).

Still, he was sanguine saying, "What's new, kitten?" and simply gave me a digipeck when I replied, "Meow don't know, puppy-wuppy."

This time, when I tapped Mark-IV, all he would say was "You need to be here tomorrow afternoon at 12:47," K-karl being a notorious stickler for punctuality.

So I tapped Harold's assistant, Orangery, and asked her to book the rocket to Paris, relieved that Harold wasn't zooming off to lunch at the exact same time.

How I longed for the day when Harold's investment in teleportation finally paid off.

I arrived, fashionably early, and Mark-IV tapped me a short presentation about "'The Fog Halo,' the greatest revolution in human fashion since the invention of the loom!"

He then ushered me into a small, bright room where I was 3D scanned, my coordinates programmed into the Halo, so I was I would not appear like some walking cumulus cloud but, in fact, a sinuous, sexy, form-fitting goddess, shrouded in heavenly mists.

Harold, who was tapped into this, kept trying to explain the technology to me, but I simply thought, "I prefer to consider it magic!"

Never one to be deterred, I heard Harold muttering under his breath something about "Ionic Nebulisation" and "Condensation Intolerance."

I was then led into the black velvet lined fitting room where I had so often met with K-karl. Even after all these years he still made me nervous, gliding in, as he did, in his thick diamond slab cube so as to avoid having to breathe anyone else's air.

I was more than a little shocked to see Grizelda, the fitting model who had been genetically altered to my exact measurements, wearing my halo and fog!

She looked stunning, of course, but my face fell for I thought I was to be the first! It took considerable effort to keep my face aloft, so this was not a happy occurrence.

K-karl explained they were in the last stages of paparazzi testing, to make sure that even the highest powered 5D flash arrays could not penetrate the "molecular envelope," as the scientists had so unromantically named it.

I must say, though, that this fitting was initially fraught with potential embarrassment. For while the fitters had seen me in the altogether, they were all women, gay, or in the case of Bobby, professionally blind, so it didn't matter.

But now I would be entering a room of men, including scientists who weren't dressed well enough to be gay and were in full possession of their faculties.

I needn't have worried, as the "SoftWear" as the marketing department was currently calling it, was a smashing success.

I was greeted with gasps and more than a smattering of applause.

As K-karl virtually pinched and tucked in the air around me, I felt the dryly viscous fog inch closer to my skin, caressing me with what felt like a warm breeze in Bali.

Now the personalized tests began, the first being dubbed, "Gale Force," named, of course, after K-karl's German Shepard, Gale, whose penchant for licking had marred more than soigne socialite. While his wet tongue on my knee gave me goose flesh, at no time did it so much as ruffle the fog.

Next, after first apologizing for making me move, K-karl asked me to walk as swiftly as I could to other end of the atelier, perhaps not knowing that I was known in some circles for being able to do the 10 meter dash in stilettos if it meant snatching the last chocolate tart at Delphine's.

As the fog tenaciously clung to me, they deemed it a success, and went to the next test they placed me in a wind tunnel and instructed that I "hold onto my hair."

As the fan spun to its highest setting, I recognized the sound as that of the Rolls Royce Zephyr jet engine on Harold's Bugatti 3000 orbital cruiser.

The wind reminded me of the hurricane force breezes on our 220th floor penthouse in Dubai during a pre-monsoon.

The fan slowed, and K-karl and the scientists, after investigating the high-speed footage, burst into cheers at my smashing success as there was not even the slightest hint of décolletage exposed.

Three months later, the Halo arrived at our personal skyscraper in Manhattan, along with a small army of technicians and instructors to prepare me for the Met Ball, the worldwide unveiling of this new sensation.

I was taught the proper way to mount it to my cranium. How to use the remote control hidden in my 20 carat pear-shaped Quadtanium ring, and how to understand the haptic feedback that would alert me to a low hydrogen situation, as well as how to recharge it with the nano fuel cell in my plutonium clutch bag.

When they were done, there I was standing in my shimmering gossamer fog. Wafting down the stairs to my awaiting chariot, only then realizing that I was going out into public —naked, at the mercy of technology and several small cartridges of nanocarbon gas.

Despite it being fall, with a touch of chill in the air, I still felt a trickle of sweat down my back, knowing that when the chariot door opened, it would feel as if I would be walking into the world spotlight, nude.

I arrived. The time came. Eduardo opened the door. I was sweating. I never sweat so K-karl had not thought to test for this. The fog disappeared.

12

again

Mom's making breakfast. She's whistling the 1812 overture, banging pots and pans for the cannon sounds.

She sounds happy.

It's weird to be back. Back in my old room. Makes me feel like I'm 12 again. Last time I saw it. 10 years ago.

She was never this happy when pa was around. Maybe she was never this happy with me around, because when they split he took me and said she didn't want me.

But she was happy to see me last night, she cried.

I'm not sure how I feel.

I know my father was a lying drunk son of a bitch, that's something I know for sure. I don't know about mom. Did she really not want me? I didn't ask her last night, I was crying, too, more out of confusion than anything.

Cillian's still asleep in the other bed. This probably feels normal to him, he talks to her every week.

I hadn't talked to her until last night.

With pa, I always made breakfast. He'd push me off the sofa bed in the living room at 6am and I'd go to the kitchen and start to scramble some eggs. One time I burnt the sleeve of my pajamas on the stove, I wasn't even awake yet.

He'd tell me how lucky I was to be with him, unlike Cillian who was with mom. He was keeping a roof over my head and they were probably homeless. Sometimes I cried myself to sleep thinking about that—I'd wish they were here, we could all sleep on the sofa bed.

But I didn't know where they were. Maybe they were dead.

Pa and I never got along, I'd do something wrong and he'd hit me and when I got big enough I hit him right back, which was easy when he was drunk. I knocked one of his teeth out and I thought he'd kill me but he was proud.

He still tried to hit me but I took boxing at school and I was good, so he never landed a punch. Didn't stop him from knocking me to the floor, though, and we'd wrestle until he passed out.

I liked fighting with dad, at least he gave me some attention other than calling me a pussy or faggot, neither of which I am. I like girls.

When he was really mad he'd say to me, "Your mother must have fucked the pussy postman and that's where you came from!"

And I wished that was true. I didn't want to think he was any part of me.

Then one morning he didn't kick me off the bed. I slept until 10 and wondered if he'd come home.

The day before I'd gotten my ear pierced, all my friends did. We got drunk and went and did it—the left ear, cause, you know. Then I came home and he saw it and called me a faggot again, and I yelled, "I LIKE GIRLS YOU MOTHERFUCKER—and you didn't even fuck my mother to get me."

I expected him to lunge at me, knock me to the floor, try to beat the crap out of me, but instead, he just sat there like I'd hit him in the head.

He started to cry, not just tears crying but blubbering and put his head in his hands and he sat there, bawling.

I'd made him cry. He'd made me cry plenty and I'd dreamed of the day when I could. At first I was proud, good for me, made the old asshole cry, now you know how it feels, fucker!

But then he didn't stop. And I started. Shit, I didn't like this. I really must not be his son, because I didn't like making him cry. I wanted to put my arm around him, the way I wanted him to put his arm around me. I wanted to say I was sorry. But instead, I just stood there, crying.

I stopped myself and wiped my face with the back of my hand.

"I'm too good to be your son." I said, thinking I could still be mean, I could do it, I could hurt him even more.

He stopped crying, and I thought, "Yeah, now he's gonna try and hit me," but he didn't. He just looked up, his eyes wet and red, looking pathetic, not just drunk but really sad.

He said, "You're right."

I blew my nose and the stench of cigarettes hit me, I'd gotten so used to it I didn't smell it anymore, but there it was, like this wall of smoke.

"I tried all this time to make you like me," he said, quietly, like he was talking to somebody else. So I'd feel like you was mine. But you was too smart to be like me."

It was kinda like he was speaking another language, like his Irish when he was mad, because I didn't understand what he was saying. It had to be an insult, he must be mocking me, so I repeated his words in my head to make sense of them.

Then he said the hardest thing.

"I'm sorry." and got up and went to bed.

From the other room I heard him yell, "I'm sorry—son."

He'd never called me 'son' before. Hadn't he ever noticed that I looked just like him?

I couldn't stay there. I went down to the bar to see if any of my friends were there but it was a Tuesday, they had to go to bed early for school, so I just sat on the curb, between the wheels of the F-150's, listening to people come and go. Wondering what it would be like to *not* be me.

It started to rain so I went home and opened the sofa bed and lay down, my head pounding. Why wasn't the asshole snoring?

Then I woke up and found him dead.

I called "pa" and I shook him but he was cold.

I didn't even know how I felt. I mean, I was relieved, but sad and scared and confused. I pulled out the bottom dresser drawer and found the metal box where he hid his money, $1,200. I took his keys and wallet and I left.

I drove north, using his credit cards to pay for gas and cheap motels. I wasn't even sure where I was going for a while but then I saw the letter Cillian wrote me, at the bottom of the box of money. Dad never showed me.

I hadn't seen C since I was 12 and he was 14. But his letter was nice and said I could come and visit him anytime in Portland, so there I was.

I knocked on the door, ready to punch him if I had to. But he didn't answer. It was a pretty black girl, said her name was Tamika, Cillian's girlfriend.

Cillian gave me a big hug, said he was happy to see me. I told him dad was dead. He said, "Good."

C looked a lot older than I remembered him. He said I did, too. He said their roommate had just moved out and I could stay in his room. He got me a job at the head shop he managed and I paid for rent and groceries and I felt like a man.

I met a girl, Amber, who was making leather belts and she needed help so I helped her then she decided she was going to move to Nashville and be a singer. So there I was, making belts and selling them at street fairs by myself.

C introduced me to his tattoo/piercing guy. I got a bar in my ear and a tattoo of the Statue of Liberty with a yo-yo—my symbol of freedom.

C and Tamika and I went to concerts—like Russell Stiltskin, a very cool retro futurist folk band. Or Pod, a set of twins who strapped themselves to each other in honor of conjoined twins and sang songs of political unity.

Then there was the K-pop hair scream band, Craptan Klunsh. I had a drink with the lead singer girl, Mary. She was really cute, all Hello Kitty but with a mohawk, and she really liked my belt so I gave it to her, even though I had to hold my pants up all the way home.

C and I were totally cool with each other, cool guys with lots of cool friends. It was a life I never knew I could have. I wasn't at all like dad.

Then C said ma wanted us both to come to Astoria for Thanksgiving. I wasn't sure I wanted to go. He said ma was cool and missed me and she hadn't wanted me to go with dad, he just took me.

That's not what pa said. I knew he was a liar but I'd believed him.

Then I saw ma, and I didn't know what to believe.

Now she's downstairs, making breakfast and whistling. My old Star Wars Death Star is on the shelf next to R2 and C3PO. She didn't throw them out. Maybe she didn't throw me out, either.

Portland's cool. I don't want to have to leave here again.

Samurai Sunrise

This is.
The last time I will see this view.
The last time I will smell Keiko's neck.
The last time I will feel the warm fragrant
water as she bathes me.

I will not return here.
This is what I tell myself,
so I do not grieve what I shall be losing.
I do not tell her. I comfort her and lie and I
say "I will return to you."
It is a lie that I would like to believe myself.
But know I must not.
For I must not sacrifice my duty for my love.
I hear her, boiling water, making soup for
breakfast.
I smell the simmering seaweed.
She will return to dry and dress me.

I will smile and look reassuringly.
Wishing to remember the contours of her
face,
the touch of her fingers,
the light in her eyes.
So that I might take this with me,
Into battle.

But I dare not.
I must deprive myself of memories.
Of feeling.
Even love.
For if I am not willing to sacrifice myself,
then I am not doing my utmost to protect
her.
And my shogun.

I will remove remembrance.
Look ahead, sharply.
But it is warm with the stove under the table.
It is warm with her hand on mine.
And the soup and tea are warm.

Soon all will be cold.
Out of necessity, even out of desire.
This is what I have promised to do with my
life.

Should I return, at least without total victory,
then I would be ashamed, damaged,
unworthy of her love.

This is why I do not plan to return.
Because, while I must dream of victory,
victory without sacrifice is only a dream.

She throws her arms around me.
Clings to me.
I bury my nose in her neck.
She has always smelled like cherry blossoms
in the snow.

I feel her tears, wet on my skin.
I keep from crying, embracing her as if she
was already a widow.

The morning light comes, I hear footsteps.

They are coming for me.
For me to lead them.
To lead them to victory.

I push her away, gently.
Nod to her.
Looking past her so the last image of her face
does not stay in my memory.

I want nothing to live for, so that I might die
for her.

The sky is pink, like her skin.
I hear birds sing, as sweetly as her voice.
As we march,
I hear gravel beneath my feet
sounding like her gentle sweeping as I sleep.
I beg my heart to stop this torment.
I will my mind to forget her love.
My love.

My men are asking, "Will we ever return
home?"
I hope they will.

But I must tell them they will not.
I can see their eyes dim.
In their hearts they have gone back home.
To their families.
For one last time.
A place I do not allow myself to go.

I cry out to them and they are forced to
return to the moment.
Their hands on their sheaths.
Muscles tensed and at the ready.
Eyes alert.

I see men approaching.
Men who, like us, wish they could have
stayed at home this morning.
And, like us, will kill for the pleasure of
returning.
I am strong, and swift of sword.
I dispatch six men.

Three of mine fall.
I whisper to them of the beauty they will see.
Their families shall not be forgotten.

I close their eyes. Take their swords.
And leave them for the animals.

While I am a warrior at heart, I still cannot
help but wonder.
Why must we do this?
As I irresponsibly think of Keiko, looking out
on the fields.
Waiting for my return.

Bird Pillow

I'm alone now because of a throw pillow. Margie and I lived in Dublin since we was born. Lived there for almost 6 years of marriage, the first three years in her parents house, then once we had saved enough money, in our own little house made of stone.

The house had sat empty for nigh 40 years and I spent my time after work and on Saturdays and Sundays rebuilding it meself—

hewing the beams, pegging the timbers, filling the walls with straw, building the lath and applying the plaster. Even finding windows at the salvage yard and re-pointing the sashes. All meself over a period of almost two years.

We moved in and things was fine, more than fine, twas a little slice of heaven on God's green earth. Hearth and home and family, even if Margie couldn't have babies, we had each other.

But soon after we moved, her mother, Agatha, arrived to inspect our new home, and she brought with her what she called a "house-warming gift."

It didn't seem very warm to me, it was a pillow, a dark blue rough burlap circle with an odd yellow bird she had clumsily embroidered on it. "With me own hands," she told us proudly, as if her hands didn't look like a witch in a fairy tale.

She placed the pillow smack dab in the middle of the settee. "A place of pride" Margie called it, so I guessed she was proud

of it, too. The sofa, bought from a church
sale, had once been red, now faded to a kind
of pink. The blue and yellow pillow felt ugly
to me eye.

Margie showed her friends like it was
something special, but to me it was a
carbuncle—always under me ass when I tried
to sit down.

And if I did sit on it, Margie would cry, "No,
dear, not on the bird pillow!" as if I had sat on
a living, breathing bird of whatever kind that
ugly yellow thing was supposed to be. If I
moved it, then she would give me a
disapproving eye, as if somehow I had taken
over that place of pride" where the pillow
was meant to be.

So I would sit to the left or right of it, where
the stuffing was thin and I could feel the
springs, while the fecking bird got the part of
the settee with the padding.

Still, it were a minor inconvenience in our
little Eden. But I did not realize it was the

worm in the apple in the garden. Not just a worm, the serpent.

But that bird didn't stop at being a snake, oh, no, it was also the piece of sand in the pearl causing things to grow around it. How a small stuffed circle could do so many things at once made me start to wonder if, rather than being "house-warming," it was really "house-cursing."

After all, Margie's mama had never been too keen on her marrying a mere craftsman like myself. Never mind that I built our house, or that Agatha expected me to come to her house to make repairs, with nary a "thank you very much."

Soon Margie comes home with another pillow. At first I was relieved to know it did not come from her mother, but from another church sale. This one was green and had a kitten on it.

"Aren't ya worried the kitten will eat the bird?" I joked with her when she put the pillows side by side on the settee.

"Angus, I'll mind the building to you and you'll leave the decoratin' to me." she replied, without the hint of a laugh.

Now there was one less place for me to sit on the settee. Just the spot on the far left, and, I began to notice, no room for her to sit next to me. She would sit on the cozy brown chair, and I was now cozying up to a kitten.

Soon it seemed like every day I would confront some new piece of frippery. Little white statues of children who looked pale as angels but with big devil eyes. Or a teddy made of little square pieces of fabric with flowers on it, like its fur had fallen out and it was trying to cover its nakedness with petals.

Then dolls with shiny black eyes that were always lookin' at a person in such a ways as to make them think they done somethin' wrong even when they ain't.

And each time Margie would say, "It's nothin'! We was gonna tithe to the church anyways, might as well get something to show for it!"

She was doing this and that in town, helping elders with shopping and cooking and she never asked for more household money so I could not complain—or so she explained to me when I found a very large red satin rose in the middle of the bed.

"Charmin' ain't it?" she said, as I struggled to find a place to lie down before dinner. I had given up on the sofa which now was home to:

- The hateful bird
- the nasty kitten
- an evil owl
- a vile Victorian girl in a pink frock
- the fecking flowered bear
- an awful orange rectangle with something I guessed was a mongoose
- and three prickly pin cushions, complete with pins

The brown chair, where Margie once sat (she now only seemed to Hoover around, endlessly, noisily and tirelessly fighting 'dangerous dust') was now home to:

- a terrible trio of cushions with chickens of various sizes, the smallest a nest with two eggs and on chick

- a sinister baby doll apparently being raised by fowl
- what I can only suspect was supposed to be a dog with matted black and white fuzz
- and on the back of the chair, another teddy that would tumble to the ground should I dare to even approach *him* as Margie took to calling it.

There was simply no room for me. Yet, somehow, when Margie's lady friends would arrive en masse, they would coo and bill over the endless array of fabric critters, and even find places to sit among them without disturbing a tableau.

"See, my friends love my sense of decor," Margie told me one evening when I was loath to find a place to sit.

"They're ladies. They're petite and can therefore position themselves…" I started.

"Nonsense, Angus. Don't be a silly dog. You could sit perfectly well if you did it like a gentleman instead of an oaf."

"An oaf?" The very word I had heard her mother use of me on more than one occasion?

"My darling, this oaf, as you call me, is your husband," I said, then not content to leave it there, "your lord and master!"

"I am all too well aware of that, *my lord*," she said, turning on her heels and sweeping into the kitchen—and out the door, me dinner with her. When it was clear she was not returning, I made my way to the pub for fish and chips, something that always gave me indigestion, then returned home, with some wildflowers I had picked as an apology.

Then one day I comes home from working and I go to lie on the bed, and in my place is now:

- a selection of satanic satin seashells looking like they had sat on the seashore a wee bit too long
- a ratty red corduroy crab
- and a shitty starfish encrusted with bottle caps of Ruby's Red Ale"

"Margie!" I shouted, "I am moving these Gawd awful geegaws!"

But before I could even grab a crab and send it flying out the window, Margie was at the door.

"If you touch a single thread of those precious pillows, Angus, then you will be making your own dinner!"

It took me a while to come up with a reply to that, so shocked was I.

"And where am I allowed to lay myself, my dear?" I said as nicely as I possibly could as my stomach rumbled in fear of eating something from a tin.

"I just hoovered the carpet, Love, why don't you give it a lie down."

"ON THE FLOOR LIKE A DOG?" I said, well, perhaps more than said, perhaps shouted with such force that I thought I saw the starfish scurry.

"It will be good for your back my dear. Besides, you are sweaty from work and should not be lying on the bed anyway, which is what your new pillow friends are reminding you of."

Well, I'll be damned if these satin souvenirs of someone else's life were my friends. But I was hungry and had been complaining about my back, and I knew Margie's carpet would be cleaner than anyone else's bed, so I wriggled down between the window and the bed frame.

I was rather cozy... except for one thing. I wanted a pillow for me head.

"MARGIE" I said, not yelling this time, well not exactly, "I need a pillow!"

For what?" she answered from the kitchen.

For what? For WHAT? For something useful as opposed to just taking space! That's what I thought!

"For me head." what's what I said.

"You don't need one."

Wait? What? I don't need one? She needs them but I don't!

I felt my face flush and covered it with my hand before angry words escaped.

Good thing, too, because Margie called me for dinner. At the dining table, she announced, "Angus, if you insist on being useless and prone, then you must first take a bath, as any civilized man should do."

But I was so tired when I got home I'd earned a lie-down. Fine, from now on, I would bathe first.

So, the next day I got home from building a greenhouse for Dr. Worthington, and I said, "Margie, I am taking a bath."

And I do, I get right in the bath. I turn on the tap, knowing it will take some time for hot water to come, but the water keeps getting higher and I get colder and the hot water never comes.

"MARGIE!" I yell. Did you pay the gas bill?" I asked, well, maybe not ask, more like shout. Much more like it.

She arrived at the door, shielding her eyes. "Of course, I paid it, Angus. But I took my bath not an hour ago and you know how slow it is. I'm off to the greengrocer," she said, in passing, disappearing as quickly as she had arrived.

Now, pardon me French but, "What the bloody hell?" She had all day to take her bath but she waited until so late she knew there wouldn't be any hot water for me?

I tried to imagine the icy water as "brisk and invigorating" but I couldn't stop shivering so I was out quickly, drying off and ready for me lie down.

But then, to my horror, the seaside tableau had grown, and now included a velvet porpoise and a ceramic clam with a light bulb inside pretending to be a pearl. I followed the electric cable and saw it replaced the light on my end table I used for reading before bed. Did she expect me to crouch by a clam to read Charlie Dickens?

I spied a small piece of paper wedged between two creatures. It was a note from

Margie: "Angus, I made room for you between the porpoise and the albatross."

Oh, that was sweet... except, I could detect no space on the bed wide enough for anything wider than her note! Being more than slightly three-dimensional myself, there was no room for me! On me own bed!

This was the last straw, the very, very, very last straw. Still in the altogether, I stormed into the living room and grabbed the accursed bird pillow!

I stomped to the bedroom and, wielding the pillow like a machete, scattered the sea creatures to kingdom come, or at least the floor, yanking the clamshell's cord out of the wall and hurling it out the window.

Ah, space.

Sweet space.

I lay on the soft satin duvet and breathed a sigh of relief.

Then I placed my head right on the bird pillow, as if it was... a pillow!

This is how I fell asleep, awoken by Margie's screams.

"ARE YOU DAFT???"

What had I done? I couldn't remember, my slumber was so deep.

"OH, YOU BEAST!" she cried, I thought at first it was because I was fully naked in daylight, so I reached down and covered me privates with a starfish.

But no, that twasn't it.

"What kind of animal sleeps on a throw pillow!"

"A tired one," I said, feeling proud of myself for finally taking a stand.

"Oh, really? Is that all you have to say for yourself, Angus?"

Despite it being one of those times when I was fairly certain she wanted me to say something else, I was fairly uncertain as to what she wanted me to say.

"No, I..." I was trying to think of what she wanted to hear. Ah, yes! "Your mother made a lovely pillow." I said, proud of myself for knowing exactly the right thing to say.

"Not for you to put your greasy head on! She's been right about you all along, Angus. Get your clothes and get out."

Me mouth was open but nothing was coming out. Was the woman actually sending me out of me own house? Was I being replaced by pillows once and for all?

Her answer came, surprisingly, with a strong volley of sea life thrown with startling accuracy at me privates. I grabbed some pants and a shirt and jumped out the window before she was able to catapult the clam.

I hid in the bushes and watched as she arranged the pillows back on the bed. I thought, "She'll get over this, she's a forgivin' kind of gal."

Then, soaring above me head, was me one good plaid suit. Three shirts. A pair of pants. Seven Socks. Four Underpants. And a pair of shoes which landed short, right on me head.

She sat on the edge of the bed, cradling the bird pillow and talking to it. I couldn't hear what she said, but in later years when I would sneak around and look in through the window, there it would be, on the settee, where I used to sit.

A Life of Things

I'm taking it down to the studs. That's the only way. I don't want any trace of what happened here for 22 years.

Nothing. None of the screaming or laughing. None of the crying or joy. None of the love. None of it.

Roger would understand. He understood every time we moved. I couldn't bear to live in a space that had traces of the last owner. Everything has to be new: new walls, new flooring, new ceilings, new fixtures and finishes and furnishing.

I'd sell some of our old stuff to clients and they'd be thrilled, as they well should have been, to have a Patric Manarö original.

But there were certain things I always kept. Things that were mine. My bed. My clothes. My tableware. My rugs. My objects d'art. Things I wouldn't share with the world. No, ours. Our things. Roger and mine, together.

But now it's time to leave this place and clean the slate for someone new to live here. I won't let them have my memories and everything here has a memory. The bed where we slept and made love. The table where we ate and entertained. The cups that touched our lips. The carpet that cushioned our bare feet with the radiant heated floors warm as it rained outside.

These are all my things, our things. Not that Roger needs them anymore. Not that he can use them.

He's gone.

So I will pack up all these things, all these memories, and I will bring them with me to someplace new. From a single story vineyard house to the 26th floor, overlooking San Francisco bay. A new place with all my old, comforting things.

I've planned where everything will go. The Matisse, in the entry, to be savored every time I come home. To an empty home... Not empty, full of beautiful things we collected together. Each one vibrating with memories of his touch.

Now it just remains to remodel away all traces of our life here. So I stand, in the middle of the living room, and I look through the wall of French doors I had installed towards the infinity pool. And for the first time in my life, I cannot for the life of me see what to change in this room.

It is perfect. The windows are precisely placed to frame the views. The entire wall of them slides back to turn the living room al fresco. The heathered cream sofas pick up hints of colors from the vineyard. The Turkish carpets, custom made to my design, echoing the out of doors. The variegated alabaster fireplace, sliced so thin I lit it from the back so it literally glows.

Perfect.

I can't touch a thing.

I can't move a piece. Doing so would defile the memory of what we created here. The perfection we created, together.

Everything we could control, we did. The lighting, the music, even the olfactory senses from flowers and incense. Ourselves, as well, fit and toned in our own gym. Everything organic, simply prepared.

Everything was under our control except for the cancer. And no amount of exercise, organic, holistic, acupuncture, meditation, or even prayer could stop it. No amount of wishing or crying or sunlight or air or

Wedgwood or Baccarat or cashmere or Matisse.

Watching him wither away, the beauty drained from his body, but not his soul. No. That—that is in my heart. That is in this room, this house.

Yet I can't stay here. I can't see him, all around me, everything I touch, without him here. The memories are thorns on roses.

So, there is only one thing I can do. I must leave everything here. Every last fiber of it. Every fork, every champagne flute, every pillow, every painting.

While I am loath to let anyone else touch it— it is what Roger would want. It is what I, as a designer, should want. To share my vision and beauty. To share Roger's memory.

I will leave with the clothes on my back. With the silver keychain Roger had made for me, of Poppet, our pug. I can feel it between my fingers every day. And remember.

The last thing he said was, "Move on." And I shall.

But I will always look back on the things we had.

Mumsy's Angel

Do you know why mumsy got custody of you, darling? It's because your daddy is an arse.

Can you say it? That's right, "daddy is an arse!" Good girl!

And you must say that, whenever you see him, because that's what he is and we call people what they are.

So when you see him, in a few minutes, you will say, "Daddy, you are an arse," say that again with me, sweetheart. "Daddy..." that's right, "You are an arse!" Yes! lovely! Louder! "Daddy you are an arse!" Perfect!

You are such a good little girl. So smart. You got that from me, remember that, sweetheart.

Why, because, let's say it again, "Daddy is an arse!" Yes.

I'm so proud of you for having the sniffles, what lovely timing, because you know something else your daddy loves? He loves it when you blow your nose on his French cuffs! Can you do that, honey? Cuffs are sleeves, sweetheart. His long Gucci sleeves. Can you do that for mumsy, darling? Yes?

You just take the fabric... no... don't do it on my sleeve but I shall demonstrate... grab it and blow... daddy loves that, especially from younger women.

And do you know why your daddy left you? And me. Both of us, all alone. With each other.

"Daddy is an arse!"

Yes my darling! That's correct. Oh, you are so smart!

But it's also important to remember that daddy does not love us—he doesn't love you.

Mumsy loves you! Can you say that?

"Mumsy loves me."

Oh! You are such an angel! You are the only good thing that has come out of my union with that swine. My precious little angel.

Now, there's one more thing we should do. Do you remember that way you used to scream if mumsy didn't get you what you wanted. You don't do that anymore because you're a good girl. That's right. You don't do that with mumsy.

It's not just because mumsy said she would give you to poor people who would buy your shoes at Walmart. I know, I know, that was a horrible thing to say, but it was necessary.

You stopped because mumsy's ears are very sensitive and it gave her a headache and you don't want to hurt mumsy, because mumsy is the only person in the world who loves you and takes care of you. Yes? Yes!

But daddy—he loves screaming. I know he loves it because I came home to find several of his girlfriends making similar sounds.

Now—you must remember that whatever mumsy does not like—daddy likes! It's like you—daddy does not like you—but I *love* you!

So anything I've told you *not* to do because I don't like it, that's what you *must* do with daddy because he will like it, because, let's say it together, yes, *"Daddy is an arse."*

Oh, my precious little princess!

I'm hoping that you're young enough so you won't remember any of this when you're older.

But what you will remember is that daddy no longer wanted to have anything to do with us and therefore must be encouraged to increase our spousal and child support accordingly.

Then you will never have to buy shoes at Walmart. Yes, like the kind Rosa had, made out of one piece of plastic that smelled like cling film, no you didn't like those, I don't think anybody actually does.

Oh, sweetheart, no, don't blow your nose yet. Wait till you see daddy and his sleeves.

All right! I want you to sit in my lap for a minute and hold you and tell you that you're the most important thing in my life. That I love you with all my heart and soul and I always will. And that your daddy doesn't.

You're always safe with me, sweetheart, so if daddy doesn't give you what you want and you're screaming and he seems upset because he's so easily upset by strong women apparently, then you just tell him you want your mumsy.

Then I will be there—because I shall always be there for you, sweetheart. Always. In fact, I'll be just around the corner waiting for you to call.

Oh! I look at you—and you're like a gift sent from heaven. Literally my little angel.

Now run to daddy, run very fast, and jump on him hard and scream loud into his ear to show that even though he's an arse who doesn't love you, that he still has a fiduciary responsibility for you—us. And that mumsy loves you.

Go! Go little angel, fly!

in my bed

Momma warned me about this. "Don't let nobody in your room, Clareese."

But I didn't let him in, he just came in.

So I played like I was asleep, like I didn't know, but I knew.

Like I knew when he got into my bed. On top of the covers, but he wasn't supposed to be there.

The moon was big and I made my eyes look closed but I squinted so I could see. He was all hairy.

And I still played asleep, maybe he just wanted to sleep hisself and would leave me alone.

He moved closer to me.

He smelled like taco chips.

He looked soft.

I was cold.

I could see his eyes. They were open and he looked sweet. Cuddly, even. And warm, I could feel him being warm.

So I turned over to look at him, right in the eye. He got scared and jumped down onto the floor and froze. I put my hand down to show him I was friendly like.

I could feel him touch me, his hair tickled.

He got back on the bed. His nose up to mine. I wasn't afraid.

I reached out, real quick, and grabbed him. He squirmed a little but then was OK. He was very soft.

"I'm gonna call you Charles," I told him, as I put that rat under the covers and cuddled with him.

She Loves Me

"What do you want?" He says it in that flat tone of his where I can't tell what he's thinking. How can I possibly tell him what I want when I can't tell what he wants?

"I don't..." I start to say, but stop. Maybe I should think about what I want. Maybe this is a good time for that, what with football season just about to start during which time I'll be busy making snacks and watching games with him, too busy to think probably.

So I think about what I want.

Well, of course what I want is for him to get down on his good knee and say, "Sally, I love you, will you marry me," and hold up at least a 1 carat flawless round (not square and gosh forbid not heart-shaped) diamond.

That's what I want.

But I also want for him to know that's what I want! What the fudge is wrong with him that it isn't obvious?

Doesn't he have married friends who are telling him what to do like my married friends are telling me? Doesn't he have a father or mother who'll sit him down and say, "Aaron, you've been dating Sally for three years now, it's time..."?

Was he raised by wolves or Unitarians? I don't get it.

So I can't tell him what I really want, because he needs to know on his own. Otherwise, every time I show my friends the ring and they ask, "How did he propose," I'll be saying, "I told him to take us on a sunset cruise..." and they'll all look at each other the way we all looked at each other when Marie showed us her sad little possibly not even real diamond heart-shaped ring from the mall, and said Brad proposed in the back of his pickup. Ick.

No, he has to figure it out on his own.

"I want you to figure it out on your own," I say to him.

He rolls his eyes. He's always rolling his eyes at me, and it's amazing I can even see that because they're so small.

"I'm not a mind-reader, Sal," he says, rolling them again.

I don't know what to say to him because he won't say anything to me.

So I pick up my phone and pretend I have a text message from Deb, my pretty much mostly best friend who I've known since I was six, though I hated her until we were nine and ended up in the ER together because her mom was drunk and ran a red light during carpool and we both got broken arms. Then we became best friends, pretty much for the most part.

I text Deb, "Call me now and tell me it's an emergency!" and I know she will, because she's obsessive about her phone, which she calls "Swarovski" as if that's exotic because of the Swarovski crystal case she got on eBay. Then she named her car "Hutch." Sheesh.

I also know that even if I do get her alone she'll spend all her time texting unless I get her somewhere with bad AT&T reception, and the only place I know that's less than one bar is "La Petite Auberge," which is kind of pricey but kind of worth it if I expect to be able to hold a real conversation with her.

She calls. Sobbing. What a drama queen, but it is nice and loud so I can wave the phone at Aaron and he can hear.

"It'll be OK, honey," I say, loud, in case Aaron has been distracted by an F-150 commercial which is all he's talked about lately. "Of course I'll meet you at Auberge at 3." I put hand up and tell Aaron, "I'm sorry, hon, I really have to go, she's in crisis."

He rolls his eyes. Again. He thinks Deb is a total flake because she's always in crisis because I'm always having to text her when I don't know what Aaron wants me to say.

I give him a peck on the cheek. Ug, it's stubbly again. He needs to shave twice a day. I've told him and he doesn't care. He comes home, smelling like tar from his roofing job and has to take a shower anyway but the tar smell never quite goes away.

I dash to my Bugster, top down, Van Halen's new album of Broadway tunes playing. Their latest singer, I can't remember his name, does a good David Lee Roth impression and sounds great singing "Memories" from Cats, which I sang in the Brookhurst Civic Light Opera three years ago, which is where Aaron saw me because his mom had season tickets and his dad refused to miss one of the semi-final games of whoever it was. It was fate!

I'm at Auberge five minutes til, I always like to be a little early, like it's an audition, and there's nobody there, except for Andy... well, Andre as he likes to be called at work where he puts on a French accent.

But I know him from "Cats" so I know it's an act, though a sexy one. I put on my French accent, as if we're two Parisians, somehow lost on the streets of Brookhurst Indiana. LOL. Makes me laugh every time.

He kisses me on both cheeks, and his cheeks are so smooth. If he can do it, Aaron certainly must be able to.

He joins me at what I like to think of as my booth, which is in the window so passersby can watch me. If it was night the overhead light would shine dramatically on me, like a spotlight, but now it's just sun and a little hot.

I've always liked Andy. If I hadn't just known he was gay I would have made a move on him ages ago. Even though he's not much of a dancer, he's dashing and funny and has a lovely baritone voice. Ah, all the good ones are gay.

"What smells so good?" I ask him.

"Me, I put on some cooking sherry."

We laugh, I smell his neck. It's a lovely neck. Why do the gays get the best necks. And arms. And pecs. It's not fair.

"Are you gonna audition for Cabaret?" Andy... Andre asks, making "Cabaret" sound especially lovely and French.

"Um, no. Probably not. I don't know. I'd like to..."

"You'd be a perfect Sally," he says, smiling with all his lovely, straight, white teeth. At least his teeth are *straight!* LOL.

And how sweet of him to say that. "Just because my name is Sally..."

"No, you've got the voice and you've always been such a great dancer."

Well, I have to tell you, flattery will get you everywhere in my book and he was looking right in my eyes when he said it and I knew he wasn't BS'ing me.

"That's very sweet, An... dre, but I've retired from the theater," I said, saying the word "theatre" with an English accent because it always sounds best that way.

"It's the theatre's loss," he said, noticing a customer entering and giving me a little wave as he lithely dashed off to greet them with his perky little ass.

Aaron never said things like that. He didn't even like *Cats*, the show, or the animals, he just said I was "Cute," and looked good in my costume, which, admittedly, I did, as it was a skin tight leotard with a few wisps of hair suggesting my feline nature. And I thought Aaron's rough good looks were manly...

I snap back to the present. Sally Bowles in Cabaret. I've always wanted to play her... but Aaron has season tickets and it would interfere...

Five after and Deb's still not here, no surprise. She'll wander in around half past, by which time I will have filled up on the bread and lovely salted butter. I love butter.

Andre comes back to the table. "Where'd we leave off... that's right, you've got to audition for Sally. I'm going to audition for the MC. Wouldn't that be great working together again?"

I sigh. It would be so great. I remember how much we laughed together. All those funny pictures we'd take in and out of costume. Well, not like naked out of costume, but I wished. I even put his hand on my boobie once because by gosh he's gay and all so he doesn't care but I liked how soft and smooth his hand was.

"So has old Aaron popped the question yet?"

OMG. Seriously. Andy knows. See, it was possible for a man to know. So Aaron should have known.

"No," was all I could manage to say.

"If he doesn't soon then someone else is gonna snap you up, babe!" he says, wrinkling his nose in that cute way he does. Then he holds my hand and kisses it. His lips are so soft, too.

I close my eyes, feeling his hand and his lips... then he's gone. I see him welcoming another... oh, it's not a customer, it's Deb!

She shakes her head—still talking on the phone, or trying.

"Damn, it cut out, I'll be right back, I have to use the little girls'..."

Deb's great. She was in Cats too. She could be in Cabaret, maybe as one of the slutty girls, she'd be perfect for that.

Andre slides into the booth next to me.

"So is this a reunion or what?"

"An 'or what.' I called her here because I'm having problems with Aaron."

"Oh, good!" he says, and I can't tell if he's happy I'm having problems with Aaron or that we've decided to come here and he wants to dish.

"He was never good enough for you, beautiful," he says, raising his well-groomed eyebrows and smiling.

He's so adorable. I remembered seeing his ass when we were changing costumes and it was the cutest thing I've ever seen. Nice and little and smooth, not like Aaron's which is big and hairy like the "before" in Beauty and the Beast.

Deb comes back, her hands wet. "There's no paper towel, doll," she says to Andre, then proceeds to wipe her hands on the tablecloth.

Andre doesn't roll his big, beautiful green eyes. He gracefully slides out of the booth and gives a little bow and glides off.

I sigh.

"He's lovely, too bad he's gay."

Deb is still trying to text but it's not working. "What? Frigging Swarovski. Who's gay?"

"Andy."

"Yeah, he's not gay."

I'm sure she's confused, so I wait for her to put her phone down the table. It won't go in her bag on the off chance she gets a signal, but it has to be out of her hands before she can think clearly.

I wait.

"It's too bad Andy is gay." I finally say.

"Andy's not gay," Deb says, still looking at her phone so I don't quite trust what she's saying.

"Yes, he is. He's handsome, elegant, talented and smells good. He has to be gay."

"If he's gay he did a good job hiding it during Les Mis because he was doing it with me every night."

My mouth falls open. I am dumbstruck. For two reasons. The first was that she beat me out for the part of Fantine when I clearly have a better voice, so I always thought she was sleeping with the director, Lionel. And second, because she'd never told me this before!

"Why have you never told me this before, Deborah?"

"Because you were so gaga over Aaron and I knew if I said anything you'd just say I was being competitive, which I wasn't, I was just having fun."

"But..." I started to say before she interrupted.

"And, you would have told me that it was time to get serious like you were and I didn't want to get serious because Andy was fun, but so were Geoff and Lionel..."

Aha!

"...and I didn't have to choose so I didn't. Where's the bread?"

She raised her hand and gestured something that was either biting bread or giving head. Andre smiled and went into the kitchen.

"Maybe he's bi..." I managed to say, my mouth suddenly dry.

"Not according to anybody in Les Mis, he only liked the girls."

Maybe it was the hot sun streaming into the booth, but I was suddenly so dizzy. I put my head in my hands and then when I looked up, there he was. Andy.

"Here you go, ladies. With olive oil for Deb, and I know how you love your butter, Sal."

He remembered what I liked! I thought I was going to black out, I honest to gosh did.

Now I felt like crying. We could have had our own dinner theater by now, something we'd talked about all those nights during Cats when he wasn't having his way with me not because he was gay but I guess because he just didn't like me, even though he really, really seemed to.

He sat down next to me and held up the water glass to make me drink.

"What's wrong, babe? Drink some water. I'll open this window. That'll make you feel better."

"Why?" I was crying now.

"Because you look like you need some air."

Deb waved me off and took Swarovski outside to get a signal.

"Why?" I sobbed again.

"Why what, honey?"

"Why didn't you sleep with me?"

He put my head on his shoulder. "Because you were with Aaron and that's all you could talk about." Even his shoulder smelled nice—like clean laundry.

"I thought you were gay."

He stroked my hair. I love having my hair stroked. "I *have* been told I'm pretty..." he laughed.

Then I laughed. He lifted my chin with his soft hands and he kissed me—so gently—and with a little tongue—so soft—and he tasted like spearmint, not like pot, which was lovely.

"I've never forgotten about that dinner theater idea," he said.

Deb came back in, fuming. "No bars," she said, then she looked up. "Ooh, it's about time, even back then you were all he could talk about."

* * *

Aaron married a nice girl from Mill Creek named Judy. Her father was a football coach and she loved nothing more than making potato skins and watching the pig skin. She sent me a thank you note after the wedding.

And while they were somewhere boring on their honeymoon, Andy and I were producing our first show, "She Loves Me."

The Hamburgers Have Eyes

No, Margaret, I didn't say *sizzling*. I said *snarling*. I said your hamburger is snarling. It's also abnormally large. Larger than my son was when he was born. So I really think you should ask yourself, Margaret, is this a hamburger or some kind of alien atrocity?

Because I think if you asked yourself that, Margaret, you may be forced to admit that what you have been ingesting is not a commonplace burger, no, but actually some kind of alien life form that wanted to get inside you.

Why is this not obvious to you? I have never before in my entire life heard a hamburger snarl. Or scoot on its plate towards me with an expression as if it wanted to kill me for giving away its secrets. Just look at its face Margaret. Do you really believe hamburgers are supposed to have faces? No, of course it does not have two eyes, that's because it's not human. It only needs one all seeing eye!

I don't care how good it tastes or how expensive it was. Oh, Margaret, it's not of this Earth! The sooner you realize this the less damage it will be able to do to your internal organs, and the less threat you will pose to humanity!

Put it down, Margaret put it down, now. I don't care what it's whispering to you! I mean, really, do you think it's normal for hamburgers to whisper commands to you? Meat is supposed to be dead, Margaret. Even a living cow is not going to command you to do things, in ancient dead languages which somehow you now understand!

Does none of this strike you as just a wee bit abnormal?

Do not threaten me with that steak knife. Because I will have none of it. Nor am I afraid of the third arm that is growing out of your forehead. I simply refuse to be bullied by alien entities, at least those from outside the alpha centauri quadrant.

I know that you think I'm just some stupid human, but that's because the alien inside me is much better at hiding than the one inside you! In fact, I regret to inform you that the one inside you is quite stupid otherwise it would not be growing a third arm out of your forehead. That's a dead giveaway!

And this is why you're going to have to be killed, because otherwise humans will start to realize that we're everywhere. The only good that can to come from this is that I can eat you without being infected by that creature, whose name I now sense to be weazel with a z, like Dweezil Zappa, who, oddly, has never encountered an alien species, not even his father.

So I'm going to pick up this hamburger, with the power of my mind, and you are going to follow it, because it's telling you to finish eating it. And I can tell you all this because it's not bright enough to think of any other plan but to have you eat it and conquer the world which is never going to happen. All you're going to do is embarrass yourself and every other alien on the planet, as well as find it increasingly difficult to buy clothing as new appendages grow out of you.

So I'm really saving you a lot of unpleasantness and unhappiness, none of which would have come your way if you had at least looked at the so-called hamburger before you took a bite of it.

I realize you were hungry, dear, but honestly. Clearly it chose you because it knew that you would just put anything in your mouth, which is something we both knew when you were a teenager. Everybody talked about it. It was never a secret even though you thought it was, and I never told you because I didn't want to hurt your feelings.

Okay, follow the bouncing hamburger, yes we are leaving the barbecue, which might have been the first clue, since there is a flying saucer in the backyard, and the barbecue is shaped like the head of Jerry Garcia.

Just follow it a few doors down the street, yes it's just out of reach because now you have four legs and are tripping over them because you're not used to them. So you're moving slowly and I would levitate you but I don't want the neighbors noticing.

Okay we're at my door now you just come right in, follow the hamburger Margaret, I know you want it, I can see it in your third eye. Come on in!

And now I just have to think of the best way to kill you. I could disintegrate you but that seems like a waste. Plus, I would like to know what kind of ignorant species is trying to make a play for this planet when we've already claimed it.

So I think the easiest, least messy method, the one that will be literally simplest to swallow, will be to use my shrinking Ray and then put you in my mouth and swallow you whole with a large glass of oxblood.

Ah—you went down smoothly! Now all I have to do is let the alien life form inside me dissect you and report on what exactly you are.

Ug. That's not good. You don't seem to be digesting. The last thing I want to do is throw you up. You were wearing chiffon and that will to be a nightmare.

Oh, no! Your alien is stupid but strong. I did not imagine that purely physical capabilities might have an advantage over my own intellectually superior species.

I will flood my stomach with acids like hydrochloric and whatever else is in here to dissolve you.

Not working. Must. Take. Antacid. Drag myself to bathroom. Open cabinet. Find roll of Tums.

Swallow entire roll, aluminum wrapping and all.

Oh, that's had an immediate effect. I feel better already. Maybe your species will have a deadly reaction to calcium carbonate. Wouldn't that be convenient.

Ow. Shit. Your alien is a calcium-aluminum based life form! The antacid has given you more power! You're overpowered my internal alien and are now taking control of me! Well, this is an unpleasant turn of events.

What? You're going to integrate Margaret's fashion sense into my internal programming, well that's the worst possible thing you could have said.

Margaret's feeble mother-of-the-bride aesthetic is not something that I want to unleash on an entire unwitting planet.

In fact, I would rather kill myself than wear those marabou feather sandals she was parading around in.

So I guess it's time to go outside and step in front of an oncoming bus. I always suspected this time would come, I just thought that perhaps I would have been able to see my alien overlord take over the planet and make me the queen of it.

But, alas, that's not to be. Because I would not be a proper Queen dressed the way Margaret used to comport herself.

Yes, new alien overlord. Yes, I am your obedient, humble servant. Yes, I shall go out and buy feathered sandals immediately.

But, while I still have the will to interject, I must say this is a sad day for the universe.

i

like

my reality

straight

P lay the flag song, will ya? The grand ol' high flying one. I like that one, it reminds me of when the flag used to have 50 stars on it. Before the Trumpocalypse.

Now they're back to the original 13, at least on the USA flag. I mean, the good news is there are a lot more flags on this continent. I do love some flags. Cascadia. Texlandia, Dixie and Trumplandia.

They're mostly pretty, I have to say, though Trumplandia's tacky with the metallic gold dictator portrait surrounded by old $100 bills.

The two million sheep in that country think it's swell. They ooh and aah they discovered something magical. "Look, the gold is shining in the sunlight!" They're blinded by it. Which is perfect. For them. They have no taste.

The Cascadia flag is the best. I'm not just saying that because that's where I live. It's the best because it has that shimmering color-changing background made from optical nano-fibers. One minute it can look like new waves crashing on the shore, the next snow falling on the Sierras or a cobalt sky with drone fireworks. It was designed by my friend Jean-Claude who makes movie trailers.

It's funny we still call them movies. Nobody goes to a theater anymore, they're simply projected right into our retina. Nobody minds, that's the thing.

And it could be the Xanax in the water supply, because nobody really minds about anything. I'm not sure that's a bad thing. Now I'm not drinking the tap water, of course. Nobody rich does. If you know the right people, you can still score plain old H_2O or install hand-made spectral filters from a hidden town in Lithuania.

I have to say that even on pure H_2O the world is a better place. I think that because the xanatazation of the water supply was my proposal after the riots. We needed something, and that seemed like a good way to make everyone feel better. That and free Trader Joe's delivery.

Also the international pillow fund to give everyone those soft squeezy pillows. You'd be surprised what a difference a squeezy pillow makes. Well, you wouldn't because you've got one. It works all around the world.

Violence is almost gone, except a few pockets among the unxanatized. But those are easily treated.

Money is a thing of the past. Well, not for those who still have it, but for those who never have it. They don't need it, and everybody's happy for the most part. There are days when I think about drinking the tap water, usually after I've met these women who are radiantly happy and laugh at everything I say. They don't even care that I'm still wearing a wedding ring because I never took it off after Evelyn left.

I tried with her again, after my fix to the water supply, which was, frankly, one of my motivations for that idea. I thought she'd be more amenable. But she wouldn't stop saying I was destroying the world. Like the world wasn't already a mess. I'm doing what I can to clean up the mess. I've got the world figured out. My own mess? I don't know how,

So I go out and give talks. I put that little crawl under my name, "noted futurist, solver of problems, fixer of worlds." When I watch the replay I feel better.

I give an ever so slight smile, not too much that would indicate that I was xanaxated. Just enough to say, "Yes, I'm pleased with this world I had a part in creating. Yes, you are welcome for this wonderful time I helped create. I smile just enough so that my mouth doesn't go down at the corners, which it does when I think about Evelyn.

And yes, I've tried dating apps. I've tried the secret UnXan for people who like me, like their reality straight. But the women are either sad or angry, the side effect of not drinking the water. I understand. It makes sense to feel sadness for a world where finally everything runs smoothly, except the beating of your heart.

Creature of the Night

I'm a "creature of the night." At least that's what Brad calls me.

It's true, I do like the night better than the day, especially here in LA. First—I think everybody looks better at night, don't you? When you can't see them quite as well—yeah —that helps.

Especially helps when you're getting a little up in years and you used to have 100 watt bulbs in the bathroom and now they're 25w...

and even those seem to be casting a somewhat harsh shadow.

I also think the world looks prettier at night, with all the little lights twinkling. It's so much more gentle than the summer sun beating down, making me feel like an ant under a magnifying glass.

But summer nights are lovely! I go out in shorts, a tank top and strappy sandals and it's like the world is perfect.

I have it all figured out. I got my night job at the 24-hour liquor store. And it's right next to the 24-hour supermarket so I have plenty to choose from. I don't wake up till after dusk, then I go out into the night!

My friend, April, is always trying to invite me out to lunch and I say, "April, lunch is the middle of the night for me, I can't do that," and she's like, "But we all get together and drink wine," and I say "I don't drink... wine." Then I laugh.

The funny thing is that April never gets the joke! Sometimes she relents and goes out to dinner. And she's awfully tasty because she constantly has a high blood alcohol level with a hint of cherry and oak.

Unfortunately, she's a morning person, what with the Pilates and hot yoga, so I don't see her often.

Luckily, there are a lot of lonely night owls at the 24-hour liquor store. Like this skinny little Beverly Hills lady, can't weigh 100 pounds. She comes in every other night buying herself a bottle of vodka almost as big as she is.

Her name's Denize (yes, with a "z," I asked) and she doesn't move that fast, so I can follow her home and get the best of both worlds. Then she wonders why she's so tired.

And Brad, well... handsome, stupid, Brad. He just thinks he's got a chronic hickey! It's a badge of pride for him with his buddies at work. He calls me his little night-owl, and I say "I'm really more of a bat!" and I laugh! He laughs and says "You do wear a lot of black!"

I knew Brad was the one for me, I could just smell it. Type O negative! Oh! Nothing sexier.

On our first date he's telling me how he's such a great guy because he's always donating blood! Yes! The man for me!

He says, "You cast a spell on me, Zelda!" and I say, "Oh, if you only knew!" And again, we laugh. God, I'm so happy. I should have moved to Los Angeles 200 years ago!

i

will

follow you

I'd never seen a ghost before, so it took me a while to figure out what it was.

At first I thought it was smoke or steam, but then it started to take shape. And as it moved toward me, it appeared to have its arms extended to embrace me.

Maybe I was dreaming, that's how it felt, especially when I saw the shape of Sarah's face in the smoke.

How long it had been. yet how beautiful she still looked. How I'd dreamed of having her arms around me once again. I would follow her anywhere—even to the other side.

But her arms didn't reach around my back—instead, they wrapped around my neck. And unlike Sarah's warm touch, this was icy cold and made my hair stand on end.

What should have been Sarah's eyes were just empty sockets, her face now a skull, and instead of her rose perfume, all I could smell was putrefaction.

Her vaporous fingers tightened around my throat and I couldn't believe she would do this to me. I let out a sob and watched as it made a hole in her smoky silhouette. But it had no effect on the ever-tightening grip of her arms.

Why was she doing this? All she had to do was ask, and I would join her. I've had a bottle of sleeping pills in the cabinet for the past 12 years, ever since... and every day I thought about taking them and joining her.

But as much as I wanted to be with her, I never had the nerve to do it. And I questioned whether she would want me to. She told me she wanted me to be happy... I wasn't happy without her, so...

The room was growing dark. I gasped but my lungs burned without air. I would be with her soon.

And now her face grew beautiful again. Her hair that brilliant red I remembered from our honeymoon in the Moroccan sun. That smile of eternal love, right before she was grabbed from behind and kidnapped. I paid the kidnappers every cent I had, but it took too long to raise the money, and they had buried her alive.

I never forgave myself. Maybe that's why she was here. Maybe she never forgave me, either. Or, maybe, I prayed, she got tired of waiting.

I'm coming, my darling. I'm coming.

I could never take the pills, but I could make a peanut butter and jelly sandwich, despite my severe peanut allergy.

I'm coming.

Cookie

So listen what the crazy bitch says to me. She says she invented the blow job! She invented it, like no one else had figured out that thing can fit into your mouth.

I just looked at her like she was crazy, and she kept starin' back at me, all proud, fluffin' her hair like she was a genius or something. What'ya say to that? There's nothin' you can say to that. Mashugana.

No sense tellin' the crazy bitch she's a crazy bitch! No use tellin' her you'se been doing it since 12, taught by your Uncle Ethan. No use sayin' one time you was in the Metropolitan

Museum of Art of all places and ya saw this Greek vase and it had a drawin' of it from, I dunno, thousands of years ago. No use in tellin' her that.

Besides, why spoil her excitement, right? She thinks she invented something new. Gezunterheyt, good for her. She has the IQ of a squirrel. What do I care? What it tells me is that if she's just started she's not gonna have the skills. Could still be using her teeth for all I knows.

I got so many skills I could write a book about it. The cover could be that Greek vase to show it was classy because the Greeks is classy. I might title it something like, "A gift to the women of the world," though it's a gift to the men of the world, ain't it?

But if women just knew all they had to do was open their little pie hole, that's it, they might be able to keep their men from comin' ta see us!

Oooh. wait a sec. It's good I think these things ahead, I'm smart like that. 'Cause now

I know, if they knew the secret we might be outta business.

Naw, I'm not gonna write that book, 'least not till I retire. Cause I got secrets. I even got pictures! Yeah, if I get old and ugly I'll be glad there's pictures of me young and beautiful and in the midst of giving gentlemen pleasure.

I have always said, Ruthie, that what we do is a public service, that it's a generous gift, and it spreads love and "good will towards men in a world so seriously in need of it."

This is what a soldier said to me. Just come back from France, he did. He learned some tricks from the French ladies who were experts and explained them to me. Put me at the *head* of the class, if you get my drift.

He also showed me things he learned to do with his tongue from those ladies. I was extremely grateful for this and went home and taught Harold.

Wait—this is the book I could write that would not hurt our business. "What men can do to pleasure their women."

Naw, men don't care about pleasing their women, I gotta call it something else. Like, "Men, this is how you get more sex!" That would be a good title, men would buy that book. I like that idea a lot.

You know, one of my regulars works for a publishing company. Not exactly sure what he does. But he uses a lot of big words and has mismatched socks.

So, next time I see him, lemme look at my little book here, I've got him down for next Tuesday at noon, he's got a prime slot because he's a regular, I will ask him about my idea. See what he thinks. See what it inspires in his head, or heads. I'm funny, too, the book could be funny.

If only people knew how simple sex can be, there doesn't have to be none of this mishegas. I tell my Harold, I tell him this, and he says, "you're right, Gertie, you're absolutely right."

Harold's very understanding, but he should be given how we meet. He was paying me, so it was a professional transaction, which is what the Bureau of Internal Revenue would think if they only knew. But I'm an all cash business woman and what they don't know doesn't hurt 'em and it helps me.

Besides, it's 1952, we're in the modren age now. Harold and I have a modren relationship where I have my own entrepreneurial business and he can do whoever he likes, like the ladies who come into his tire store.

All I say is, "Don't give them too much of a discount, 'cause whatever you want you can get from me for free."

I take back what I said earlier about men not caring about women's happiness because that's not true of Harold. He knows what to do with his tongue. And he likes it. Likes it!

Sometimes, if I've had a long day I'll plop myself on the sofa and he'll get on his knees and take care of me, which, even you, Ruthie, have to admit, is very sweet of him. He's a very sweet man, which is why I like to cook for him. Because this is something the women who get tires don't do very good. They bring in cookies. What is with so many goyishe women with the cookies? They can't bring in a brisket, a nice corned beef?

He brought some of the cookies home and I said, "What, exactly, am I supposed to do with this drek?" And Harold says, "You could give them to your customers," to which I replied, "This is a very good idea, Harold." See, Harold is smart, like me.

And that is how I got my nickname "Cookie." They all call me "Cookie," a sweet thing to be known by. Mr. mismatched socks calls it a "sobriquet" which makes me more special.

Men know: they come in, I give them a treat and a cookie. If one of Harold's ladies makes a bad batch, then I bake some myself, or if I'm too beat, I go down to Katz's and get some black and whites.

They don't care, all they care is that it's sweet and that I'm sweet.

And this is something else—I need to start makin' notes for this book that I'm gonna write for women. There's one *big* secret and it's not even a blowjob. The big secret that none of these shiksas, not to mention ladies in the Tribe seem to know is they only have to do one thing:

Be nice.

Because men are like puppies, that's a well-known fact. If you're nice to them, they'll do anything for you. Then you can be as much of a bitch as you want, with the "buy me this," and "do for me that," like we couldn't do for ourselves.

And, to tell the truth, if men are like puppies, then women really are bitches. It's scientific.

But the sad part, and you know this, too, Ruthie, is that it doesn't work the other way around with most of these mashuggy dames. The man can be as sweet as pie and she's not satisfied. They don't like a man who's too nice. What's not to like?

But these gals is never satisfied. I heard some at the parlor, complaining about their husbands in bed. Who's fault is that? I've had their husbands in bed, so I know if they'd just get off their high horse they might get off. But, no, they just complain. Then their men feel rejected and come to me. I'm just one woman and look how much good I do for the world!

Still, it's sad. So sad. People don't understand that it's a transactional world. You lick mine and I lick yours and the whole world could live in peace and harmony.

Maybe I need to run for public office.

Oh, I gotta go, doll. It's 4 o'clock. Last one of the day. Then I'll go home and make Harold a nice brisket like he likes, then take a load off till he comes home and gives me what I like. Life can be so simple. Ya just gotta know what's what. I'm gonna write that book, honey. Future generations will thank me.

What a Mermaid Wants

I wept when I heard the news—tears of happiness as well as sadness. I'd always hoped that she would marry. I hoped that it would be to me, but no. And yet, disappointed as I was, I couldn't help but be happy for *her*.

It was all she ever wanted. Now when I think about it, I don't know if she ever talked about the marriage. Just the wedding—peach and lilac and lilies. That's what I heard from the first day I ever met her.

I'd been watching her for a long time. See, I worked at "The Mud Hut," a coffee shop next door to "Le Reve," the ladies boutique where she worked.

I didn't own the coffee shop, but I was a master coffee roaster, so I had skills and thought someday I'd open my own roastery.

But she didn't know that. She just thought I was some barista. She'd come in with that binder of hers, filled with pictures of flowers, cakes and dresses. I'd watch her stroking the pages like she stroked the dresses in her store when I sneaked a peek from the street.

I imagined us going to Calabash Beach back where I grew up in North Carolina. We'd be barefoot in the sand exchanging rings and kisses.

She always ordered the same thing, a skinny latte. So when I'd see her coming I'd start making one. After a while she'd sit right down and I'd bring the latte to her, with a touch of cinnamon. I even stopped charging her.

When there was nobody else around I'd nod at her and she'd nod back. I'd sit down and she'd talk about her wedding. I thought she was actually getting married.

I think the first thing I said to her was, "Who's the lucky guy?"

She snapped the binder closed, folded her hands on top of it and said "nobody yet."

The second thing I ever said to her was "I'll volunteer."

She smiled. I couldn't tell if she thought it was ridiculous or sweet. It was meant to be sweet but it felt kind of ridiculous. Who says that? Then a customer came in and I got up and made them a mocha. Every once in a while she'd look up at me and smile, and as she left, she waved.

I'd had crushes on customers before.
Sometimes they'd be consummated, right
after I locked up for the night, on top of a bag
of coffee beans. The smell of the beans and
the feel of burlap on my ass was pretty hot.

It made me feel that coffee roasting was the
sexiest thing on the planet. I mean, I'd
always liked the smell of it, the oils, the way
it fills your head so that even after you leave
the smell was still there. Something so
earthy about it.

She was the opposite of that—so sleek. Her
hair so shiny, her fingernails so perfect like
she'd come out of one of the pages in her
magazine binder. But she smelled like the
sea. It was some kind of perfume but it
reminded me of seaweed which was cool and
mermaid-like.

After a while, that's how I started to see her
and with her shiny slick black hair—as a
mermaid who'd swum up the East River.
Waiting to give her siren song to the right
sailor.

Her routine was very precise. 12:05 she'd float in, sometimes with her binder, sometimes with just one of those brightly colored purses she carried. That was another reason I thought she might be a mermaid because the purses were the color of exotic fish like you'd find a reef—coral, clown fish, yellowtail, neon tetra blue. Sometimes when she'd be searching for something at the bottom of a purse she'd almost bury her face in the bag. Then I could only see that shiny black hair cascading down till she looked up this expression of delight, like maybe she just found a little fish.

I wanted to be the sailor she'd sing to. But I didn't know how to swim. In fact, I was always afraid of water. I had dreams of drowning. And yet I would have drowned for her.

My friend, Joe, said, "You're an idiot, Sam. You don't even know this woman." I'd think, "Yeah, he's right."

Still, I knew she always closed up at 6pm, so I finally screwed up the courage to go next door at 5:58 carrying a skinny latte and said, "Hey, you hungry?"

She looked ravenous, like she hadn't eaten all day. I was worried about her, but at the same time wondered if I might be her next meal.

She said, "Sure," and picked up her salmon-colored purse, locked up and we went across the street to Giuseppe's, a trendy Italian place that was way too expensive for me, but why not? I was going to get to know her!

It was so easy to talk to her, like in a dream. And the breadsticks were fantastic, studded with Parmesan cheese and flecks of rosemary. I felt overwhelmed by the flavors in the scents—and the view of her.

I was afraid to ask questions. So I told her about myself, how I moved from North Carolina because I thought I wanted to be an actor and it didn't take long for me to realize I wasn't cut out for it. I'd fallen into coffee shops because it was a job but I realized it was also what I loved.

I loved roasting the beans. I loved making the coffee and seeing how it changed a person's day—not just the caffeine but the ritual. And how I believe ingesting that earthiness changes a person. I told her about my dream of opening my own roastery and how I love the feeling of the beans in my hand and the smell in my head and knowing I was part of this cycle like a gift to the people who drank it.

And then I realized I had been talking a lot and eating a lot of breadsticks and I felt embarrassed and probably turned red and stopped.

She said, "That's beautiful."

I could feel myself blushing, so I pretended to wipe my lips, hiding behind the napkin.

She said, "I only want one thing—To be a bride and have a wedding. That dress. That day. The way you feel about coffee beans, that's how I feel about dresses. I help women change who they are and how they feel about themselves. And I keep waiting for one that will change how I feel about myself."

Then, it was probably the wine. The bottle was $62 which was insane for me but worth it to be able to sit there and look at her and watch the candle light on her downy cheeks and shiny hair. It was the best movie I'd ever seen and included breadsticks.

But I couldn't figure her out, what would she want to change? "You seem so cool. Like you've got it all together."

And she laughed, loud, so loud people at the other tables looked. Then she put her hand over her mouth embarrassed, leaned in and whispered to me, "I'm waiting for the one that will let me live in this world."

I—ridiculously—thought she was talking about how she was a mermaid pretending to be a girl. That's literally the thought that came into my head and I felt myself nodding.

"You get it, don't you?," she said.

I nodded again. Then I said what might have been the stupidest thing anyone's ever said on a date or whatever this was. I said, "I can see... your fins."

She looked deep into my eyes. Suddenly I couldn't hear anything. No people talking. No forks clinking against plates. I felt like I suddenly gone deaf.

And all I could see were her eyes which were so dark and deep I was the sailor drowning in them.

Then she looked down and all the sound returned. I gulped for breath. I had drowned and lived. I sat back in my chair, conscious of my breathing, waiting for her to say something. She looked up at me, shyly, like I'd never seen her look before.

"You see me," she said.

I paid the bill. She picked up her salmon purse and took my hand and we walked across the street. She unlocked her store, we went inside and she locked it again.

The only light was the glow from the street lamps outside. She pulled me close and kissed me, sliding her hand down the back of my pants and wrapped her fin around my ass cheek. I was drowning in joy.

I shed my clothes and she shed her hard gloss. We flopped around on the floor, on a carpet, which I'd never noticed, that had a coral pattern. Now, I was a fish doing a slippery mating dance that felt as primal as coffee. I'd gone from never even touching her hand to feeling her skin, her iridescent scales, her soft, wet secrets.

I felt like there was lightning in my head. I could see her on the coral carpet, then on the beach with sand and underwater. I wasn't sure what was true, and I didn't care. Finally, an animalistic explosion. I felt I had made her mine.

Then, slowly, she turned back into a woman. A human woman, wrapped up with me on the floor of a shop, looking chilly. I covered her with my coat, carefully tucking it around her shoulders.

She said, "That was beautiful," while looking so sad.

"So beautiful. So why are you sad?"

"Because you gave me what I needed. But you can't give me what I want."

We didn't talk after that. Now I hear she's getting married to a rich bond trader. She's finally getting what she wants. I'm gonna stick around, just in case there's something she needs.

Me, Robot

I t was a relief to turn off my emotions. I always found them to be a pain anyway. I never knew when they might get out of control. So better to simply eliminate them.

The implant made that possible. I was a beta tester for the *EmoNo* from Control Systems. It didn't hurt that they offered a million credits because I was in pretty bad straits after drinking and gambling away what little I made working in my first Exoskeleton.

I like being an Innie… people don't think about the fact that their so-called AI robots are really people inside robot suits. The initial wave AI androids were fatally flawed, and after a series of unfortunate massacres, pure AI robots were made illegal.

Elon Musk, the force behind the creation, then criminalization of AI, realized it was easier just to pay people to wear robotic exoskeletons, which the marketing department named RoboExos, and work as an "Innie," which is what we call ourselves. Musk leases the so-called robots to customers and credits the humans inside.

The RoboExos are quite pleasant, cooled, heated, taking care of all bodily functions, from input to output—pie hole to poop shoot. The exoskeleton makes it easy to lift or move or carry anything up to 500 pounds. And the contract states that Innies can only work 8 hours at a time, then require their own private bedroom with food and bathroom to recharge. So the livin' is easy!

Nobody questions it. Even if they actually know, they just don't care what's behind the tech or inside their robot. We Innies are happy for work, most of which had already been taken by other machines.

So there's free room and board and a sense of purpose. Do you understand that? Purpose. Being able to do something useful for someone else, not just sitting around in your shipping container, using government credits on alcohol, gambling and porn.

Oh, but speaking of porn, when I first got into my RoboExo, I was a porn performer. Robot porn is really hot, I mean, it's what I watched, so why not get involved. Very athletic. They can fuck while skydiving or underwater and I was surprised how exciting it was on the inside.

But people like new models, and my suit was out of date so I went into indentured servitude. 7 years of low-paid service during which time you earn the right to own your Exo at the end... though the truth is the suits need refurbishment after 7 years and most

Innies can't afford what it costs to fix them, so we go back to working as indentured servants.

This is my third servitude, but I'm not complaining. No, I love it. Love it! The suits are cozy. I can listen to music and watch movies on my view screens even as I'm seeing the actual work that needs to be done.

And the truth is, not that much really needs to be done. People think there's a lot of work, cleaning, cooking... but if they bothered to do it, they'd spend maybe an hour or two a day at most. They've got all those little robot appliances for cleaning and cooking anyway. But the rich ones want a big strong robot to "protect them."

Most of the time I sit in my suit and watch more robo porn and suck on the nutrient straw and feel invincible.

See, that's the key. I am invincible in this suit. I can do whatever I want and nobody can stop me, except with a remote control, and then they're not really stopping me, they're stopping the suit.

So I'm finally in control of my own life— thanks to the EmoNo chip and the RoboExo!

Sure, sometimes I get really angry. Sometimes I think about killing the people holding remote controls. (Laughing).

But when that happens, the suit just buzzes my EmoNo chip and I suddenly feel calm again. I'm so grateful. Grateful for the control I have by being controlled.

World without Work

D amn, it's raining. I don't feel like getting out of bed.

I won't.

I'll just go back to sleep. Nothing important to do today.

Oh—I have Yolates. Then I told Deb and Sweeney we would go out to lunch after.

And I have court-ordered meditation. You'd think that now that we no longer have to have jobs, we could do whatever you wanted, but, apparently, drinking all day is not acceptable.

I don't understand why, because personally I find when I drink I enter a new state of consciousness! I don't see why the government should be involved in my states of consciousness! That's a violation of my civil rights!

I could look up an AI-ttorney and sue.

Uh, except that would take effort, I'm just going back to sleep.

Oh. One o'clock.

ShipShape, come! Get me ready to go out.

Sigh. I find this so tedious, it takes a full five minutes for her to clean me, make me up and dress me. I hear that the newer model can do that in four and a half minutes, and that sounds better, but I need credits for it and alcohol isn't free, so I have to decide what's most important.

Ouch that hurt, Shipshape! And that always tickles which I kind of like but it's annoying because I've asked that idiot robot not to do it.

Ooh, I just thought of a way to save credits. Instead of going out to lunch I could have the girls come here.

Shipshape, please make lunch for three. One vegetarian, one gluten free... don't you roll your eyes at me, missy. Your memory is glitchy so I have to remind you.

And you know what I want. And don't say, 'Only a martini,' don't you dare say that! You're getting awfully sassy for a bot, bitch.

Ooh! I just had a brilliant idea! If I stopped drinking long enough I could afford to trade you in for a newer model—so don't give me any mouth.

Honestly, if I had wanted a mother then I would have been born to one! That was funny, ha ha ha. I know some people still have mothers but I find that violently disgusting. I prefer the much more modern and sanitary method of Amniotic Pod Gestation.

Ooh, Shipshape come back here. What did you dress me in? Yes, I know this is a Yolates outfit, but it's pink! You know this is Tuesday, you know that Deb and Sweeney will be there, so come on and use that giant memory bank of yours and figure it out.

That's right. Deb is deathly allergic to pink. It makes her break out if she so much as sees it. The entire class has been warned. Are you trying to undermine me? I've got my eye on you, missy.

Take it off me and put on the blue one. I think you may have a screw loose.

Yes, I want lunch for three as I said. But before lunch I want you to do a thorough diagnostic, and, if necessary, have a technician visit. You're still under warranty, aren't you?

This is a formal request so you can't ignore me, you have to do what I tell you to do. I shouldn't have to remind you of the Asimovian laws, they're engraved right there on your wrist. Honestly, sometimes I think you are more trouble than you're worth.

Oooh, that was funny again, because sometimes I say that about Deb and Deb says it about Sweeny practically every day.

Wait. I'm confused about my schedule. Yolates. Meditation. Did I say they were coming for lunch? They're coming for dinner. Ooh! I have the times wrong.

Now—why didn't you notice that? You should have known it was meditation, then Yolates, then dinner. You should have listened to the way I said it!

I hope the new models can do that. Or read minds. Maybe I could get a loan from Sweeney. She sold that picture of a pickle she painted so she has extra credits.

I'm surprised no one has bought my AI paintings because they're very good. Printed on velvet. With big eyes. They're all the things the online masterclass said were commercially viable.

Shipshape I've told you not to make any comments about the placement of the ears. You did that once, you said they were too low and looked like they had fetal alcohol syndrome and I did not appreciate hearing that.

There really is something wrong with you, isn't there. I'm starting to worry.

I have a very strong maternal instinct. Of course you noticed. Deb said that to me the other day. When I said I was worried about her because she looked so tired and had big puffy bags under her eyes. Then her Shipshape gave her an avocado peel mask and bedtime icepack and she looked younger the next day.

Hmm. you're not looking very good yourself, Shipshape. You need a good polish. You can do that yourself, can't you? Of course you can, you can do everything.

But if there's some extra special polish you need that you can't do yourself, go get it. I want you to shine because you're a reflection of me. Oh... funny again! I'm positively a scream!

You can have a credit. Up to four. But only for a polish. And if you ever show me the accounts and I see you've done anything else with it you'll be punished.

And you know I mean it, because there was that night where you wanted to go out with one of your little android friends and I said "absolutely not," and you said you didn't go but I found a taxi receipt in purse and didn't remember taking the taxi and turned you off for 20 minutes until I needed something from you.

Oh, I'm so agitated now I need a martini. Shipshape you really are a lot of work, you know that? You must be what it was like to have a child.

Oh! I've forgotten to eat and you've forgotten to feed me! Wait, it's on the table? I'm in a hurry, I didn't know I had to go all the way to the table. Why couldn't you bring it to me?

There's definitely something wrong with you, you've gotten lazy. Though I do have to say this food looks lovely. You know just how I like my hopper eggs and pseudobacon. And I can tell the latte is exactly 145 degrees, that's just how I like it. So you're not completely brain dead.

What's this? Paper? You printed a letter? You know I don't like that. From David? If it's from David you should have brought it directly to me, better yet, project it to my ocular.

I don't care if he insisted it be in print.

Open it for me, you know I don't like to touch paper. It's a fear. It's a primal fear of mine. That and botulism.

Oh, so many words. Reading is such a pain, read it to me Shipshape, and use David's voice.

"Dear Starla..."

Stop! Stop! David's voice is a little deeper and a little slower. More like a man. Adjust.

"Dear Starla. You know that I have tried to develop feelings for you..."

Stop! Stop! It's hard to hear while I'm chewing. Tell me in between bites. Wait! OK. I've swallowed, continue.

"'Of late, I have been unable to...' excuse me, ma'am, there's an incoming call from Deb."

Connect me. "Hi, Deb, dear, yes, I'm having breakfast now. It seems to be the one thing Shipshape is able to do properly. I know, I've got court ordered... you don't have to remind me of these things. Meditation, then Yolates, then, for dinner I've decided we're all coming back here and Shipshape is making dinner."

"Yes, I am trying to save a few credits. No, it's not entirely for martinis. 4 o'clock, yes. I'll be as on-time as I can possibly be. If I'm not, start without me and I'll come in when I can. It doesn't make any difference, does it, why are you such a control freak, Deb?"

"I have to finish eating and each bite takes time and then Shipshape, for some unknown reason, is reading me a printed letter from David. Yes, yes, he insisted. Paper. Ew! I know."

"No, I don't know what it is yet and I resent the fact that you assume it's bad news. I will see you later."

Please continue with the letter.

"I have been unable to put out of my head the fact that we are having difficulty making a deeper connection than the one we make in bed. And while, yes, you are the best sexual partner I've had in some time, emotionally I feel my needs are not being met..."

Stop! STOP! What did he say about me being a sexual partner?

"...the best sexual partner I've had in some time."

Oh. That's nice. But I don't see how I'm supposed to meet his emotional needs. My guru says you have to meet your own emotional needs. That's not very mature of him.

Continue...

"And so, for now it's best if we don't see each other. And while I will miss your great oral skills..."

That's so sweet, isn't it?

"My Shipshape is also quite adept at this so I won't miss you that much. Thoughtfully, David. End of Letter."

Incinerate that piece of paper, I don't want it around the house where I might get a paper cut.

He was never my first choice anyway, he was just there.

OK, Shipshape, while I'm gone I expect you to search the personal apps and find someone compatible for me, if in no other way than at least sexually.

Why do you keep saying "I can take care of that for you?" I'm clearly a heterosexual human woman and as a maid you can't...

What? I thought you had that thing removed when I told you to be a maid, not a butler.

Oh! I find it disturbing you've been hiding it under your skirt all this time.

Though... I am... a bit curious... as to the color... and size...

Please show it to me now.

Ooh. Impressive.

And all this time I'd been under the impression you'd switched parts. You may have told me but you know I don't listen.

I also don't remember you telling me that you were skilled in every human maneuver, either. I think I would have remembered that, unless I was hungry or sleepy or had too much to drink.

Oh. I have an idea!

Oh. I forget you're not a mind reader. So—I'm thinking that sex might be good for you.

It's not that I want it, but I want to be helpful to you.

This might be your entire problem right here
—your sexual misidentification.

You really should have showed me that thing
early on.

OK! Move my meditation appointment,
cancel the Yolates and cancel dinner...

Bullshit & Art

Art is bullshit. Artists are assholes, just trying to get in your pants or your wallet.

Sleeping in late, drinking coffee, creating bullshit and explaining how it's genius and we should all be grateful to them so they can fuck you.

I know. I'm an artist, and what you're reading is bullshit.

In the past I would never have admitted it. Never. I'm breaking the artist's code here by telling you the truth. But art isn't about truth.

Art is literally *artifice*.

I hear other artists saying that they're "revealing the truth," a "truth that people otherwise refuse to see," bullshitty things like that.

In reality, art is about us trying to fool you. Fuck you. Yup. Like we know something special and magical that you don't.

Well... actually... we do. That's right. Or at least we did until Lois made me spill the beans.

Lois.

That's right. A woman. It's always about a woman, isn't it. In art, I mean. Even if sometimes the woman's a man.

Love and loss and all that bullshit. Who gives a fuck? Who cares that Lois left me and all she left me was a broken heart and a half a case of Jose Cuervo?

I don't care. Fine, go.

Me, I'll just paint about it, like I always do. I'll slap some acrylic paint on my ass and scoot around the canvas, like I'm an artist. I claim to be an artist, therefore I am.

I got paintings in the Hooppole museum in Illinois, and the Edmonton Museum of Exotic art, and most exciting to people who buy my shit, Lindsay Lohan has a couple of my pieces. She didn't buy 'em, mind you, I just mailed 'em to her. Same with Selena Gomez and Katy Perry and forever ago, to Cher.

But who wouldn't want to have a painting by the genius who's hanging above Gwen Stephanie's bed? Huh? Shit she gave me such a hard-on. Painted my cock and my ass and scooted around like a dog with worms and made a painting I called, "Desire in the key of C flat minor."

I don't know anything about music, 'cept I like it. And the ladies who sing it.

So, Lois gets tired of me lusting after all these girl singers. Come on. Like I'm ever gonna meet 'um much less fuck 'um?

And it's all because of that bitch Lindsey. Lohan. I get a call from a gallery saying she took the picture I *gave* her in to sell and who am I, just a guy who scrawled his number on the back and they don't know if it's worth shit.

Well, it's worth at least shit, come on, 'cause I'm sure there might be a little bit of it on my ass when I'm scootin' around, but if they mean big bucks, well, sure, why not.

And I tell them about all the girl singers, and I remember Pamela Anderson who doesn't sing but she made my cock sing so I sent her one. So it's a pretty fucking famous bunch of ladies.

And some snot nose gay boy on the other end of the phone he says, "Oh, I see." Like it's nothing. Like my entire life's work is nothing.

And let me tell you, three Cuervo's ain't enough to dull the pain of Lois and this little asshole combined.

"CHER!" I shriek like an animal in pain.

"What?" This little prick says, like I might have hurt his delicate senses.

And suddenly he's nice. "Cher!" he says, with respect.

Look, gay guys are nice, they buy my stuff— usually not because of the singers, but because they know how I make it and they think it's hot.

Fuck it, I'm hot. I've always been hot. I was the captain of the football team in high school. I was a jock. Didn't start painting until I got really drunk after college and I was trying to find a way to get backstage at a Paula Abdul concert, and I figured if I'm carrying some real live art shit, and say it's a gift, they'll let me in.

So I paint my ass and scoot around and then I'm at the backstage door holding this paintin'. It's a big 'un, too, the size of my bathroom door, because it is my bathroom door which I took off its hinges.

And they don't give a shit, because I guess they know art is bullshit, being around that "musical artist" and all.

But Paula comes out to her car, and she stops to look a the painting, and I says "It's a gift from me, I made it for you, I'm an artist, too," and she smiles and says, "Thank you, honey," she called me "honey," and points to a big bodyguard guy walking with her and he takes it from me and puts it in the back of her black SUV.

And then they're gone and I'm sobering up enough to think, "Fuck, I shoulda put my name and number on it so she could call me, and maybe hook up," but I didn't.

But now I did have my first celebrity collector. And when I'd feel down and horny, I'd think of it, hanging above her bed, watching her sleep naked, and imagining myself there next to her, inside of her, painting her ass, too, and creating art together.

That's what I imagined about all those singer ladies. Just us together, in love and art.

That's what I imagined with Lois, after I saw her set at the Blue Devil Saloon on Highway

22. Her and her guitar. In the flesh. Almost close enough to touch.

And during her break I went back to my truck and rifled through a pile of paintings I didn't sell that weekend at the Wichita Celebration of Art at Capitol Square.

And I saw the perfect one for her. Small. Square. Blue. Like her music.

I brought it in with me and put it on the chair next to me, since there weren't many people there listening, and by the end of her set, just me, and my "Blue Dawn" painting. I called it that because it was blue and it was dawn when I made it.

She goes to the bar and they give her a drink and I go up to her, just like I went up to Paula and Janet, Mariah, and Taylor, only this time there's no other people or bodyguards, and I say, "I love your music. I'm an artist, too, and I want you to have this."

Her eyes were blue and when she looked at the paintin' she smiled. They lit up, like. She sat at my table and we talked. And she asked if I could give her a lift home, and on the way her hand touched mine, and I pulled over and we kissed, right there on Highway 22, with the semis roaring by, making everything shake.

We went back to her place and made love, under the Blue Dawn. Just like I'd always dreamed.

And when she couldn't pay her rent, she moved into my trailer with me.

We were happy, too. We were. She made a mean pasta marinara, not even out of a jar or anything, but from real canned tomatoes.

We made love, and we made art. She wrote her songs and sometimes I painted her ass and we made beautiful paintings together. Those ones really did sell the best, like the people lookin' at them could just tell they were made with love. They could feel it, like I could.

But art's a business, whether it's music or painting, and we both had things to do. She went on tour as the opening act for a southern rock band called "Marked Man," and I suspected she was fucking the lead singer, Mark.

I went to art shows and there were always girls impressed that I was an artist and all, and I look good in tight jeans and a cowboy hat, so it's not like I was all alone at night.

But that wasn't even it. No. It was me sending more paintings to more girl singers. Rihanna. Beyonce. It was Beyonce that broke Lois' camel's back.

"I can't stand it, Lee. You getting off to Beyonce's "partition" song while we're making love. You thinking about her under one of your paintings. It's like I'm not there."

But she was there. I knew it was her. And a little bit of Beyonce, too. That's normal, that's what guys do.

That's what artists do. They take what is and they mix it with what isn't and they make something new—something wonderful.

We had something wonderful—And she told me it was bullshit.

She said, "And your so-called art, too. It's a joke. Bullshit. Get a real job."

My father used to say, "Get a real job," when I said I was gonna be a rock singer.

Then there was that asshole agent who told me I was tone deaf and better find something else to do. Fucker.

But he did me a favor. I found painting. I found all those girl singers. I found Lois...

Naw, it was all bullshit. Even though, when I was scooting around, I was thinking about people and things. It wasn't random like a dog, even though I said that, no, it wasn't. I was thinking about love and beauty and cancer and sausage and rent money and hunger and fear and... love.

Love is bullshit.

Wait. Who's that on the radio? Miley? She sings like she knows something I don't. I want one of my paintings above her bed.

Marlboro Man

I can't find it. My respirator. I can't. Find it. I need. it. so I. can. breathe.

So I. can. smoke.

I. I. I need. a. cigarette... light. it.

Not supposed. to smoke. Oxygen tank. can explode.

Light. headed. Another drag. on. cig. Ahhh.

Need more. oxygen. Keep look... ing around.

dizzy. puff. hand. shaking. cig falls. onto green. shag. carpet.

Lean over. dizzy. dammit. Hard to. breathe.

I see. red. glow on. carpet. Fire!

So tired. Stamp. out car... pet.

(gasp) (gasp) (gasp) (gasp)

Don't want. to put. out cig. just started. it.

Dizzy. Step back. Fall. back. Hit my. head. again...st. wall.

On my. ass. Reach. for cig. Need. respir...at...or.

Oh! My. new pack. of. marl...bor..os. under. dress...er. thou...ght. I'd. lost. 'em.

Need. air. need. cigs.

Crawl.

My. leg. feels. hot. fuck. Pant. caught. Fire!

(gasp gasp gasp)

Shake. my. leg. to put. it out. Ow! It's. sprea...ding.

Grab. pack of. cigs! Saved. 'em!

Terr...ib...ble. smell. bur...ning. plast...ic.

Resp...or...at...or mask. on. fire.

Fire. spread...ing. all. a... (gasp) a... (gasp) a...round. (gasp)

Burn...ing. the. ox...y...gen. tu...be. to...ward. the... tank.

Flip. open. the. pack. Take. one. out...

Light. it on. the. burn...ing car...pet.

Nice. long. sooth...ing. drag.

My Monster

Yes, I saw the monster behind me. He was clearly visible in the mirror, so him sneaking up behind me did not go unnoticed. I assumed he was a "he" because I doubted that a "she" would be this careless.

Not to mention that he smelled like a rotting carcass and his breath was so heavy it felt like a hot foul breeze that made the room feel tropical.

This wasn't the first time a monster had come into my bedroom. The previous times had gotten messy, and I was determined not to make the same mistake this time.

Here are a few things I learned:

1) Never scream. They hate screaming. It upsets them, they wet themselves and, trust me, there is no product on earth that will take out the smell of monster pee. You just have to throw out the carpet and start over.

2) Never look them in the eye. It makes them giggle. And while that sounds charming, and for the first few seconds I actually thought it was, it inevitably leads to them throwing up, and, like their pee, you simply have to replace anything their puke touches. This includes hardwood floors.

3) For God's sake don't pet them. I learned this the hard way. I thought I'd got it all figured out—I didn't scream, I didn't look, and so it nuzzled up to me in its furry yet repulsively sticky way. Then he (once again, it felt like a "he") started making adorable little noises, like an alligator mated with a

kitten, and something instinctive compelled me to pet the top of its head. I didn't know, until that very moment, that the top of their head was an erogenous zone... and once again I was dealing with a monstrous fluid, only this one dried and hardened within seconds which made it difficult to move.

So, tonight, I was just going to ignore it and hope it would go away.

This was easier said than done, because they do smell, and my mind kept going over the costs of new carpet, new bed frame, new flooring...

So I lay, stock still, in the bed. And I thought about all the possible reasons why my bedroom had become monster grand central.

I chalked it up to the crying over my ex, who I'd broken up with, calling him "a monster." Well, he was. At the time I couldn't think of anything more disgusting than him coming to bed after going to the gym and not taking a shower—then thinking he could get romantic. Little did I appreciate that at least I could wash the sheets, I didn't have to burn them.

But I figure the real monsters don't have a choice, they were born this way, whereas Curt was a grown-ass man and could have... no, should have learned that it was common decency to take a shower after being all sweaty.

He'd say, "I think I smell good," and I'd say, "Why would you possibly think that" and he'd say, "Because I have a nose, Lila," and I'd say, "Well, it's not working," and by this time he'd be fast asleep, then gone in the morning when I had to wash the sheets in hot water.

So finally I emptied his drawers into bankers boxes I'd brought home just for the occasion, dragged them outside and texted him saying it was going to rain and he should come pick them up immediately.

I had a locksmith change all the locks, I turned off the lights and peered through the blinds to see when he came. I wanted to make sure he was angry. I imagined I could still smell him through the double-paned windows.

And I cried. I cried because even though Curt was a monster, he was *my* monster. And if he hadn't been so disgusting, he might have been OK. No, my mother didn't like him. My friends all said he was an animal. But he kept me warm at night.

He never did pick up his shit, so it just sat there, on the lawn, getting soggy, until I had to drag the wet, smelly boxes to the curb.

I came back inside and cried, no, not cried, wailed. Because now my apartment smelled really nice and I liked it, but it was too quiet. There was no stomping around, no throat clearing and snoring and farting. It felt empty.

So, when the first monster arrived I was shocked, of course, but somehow not that surprised, perhaps because I'd become used to Curt—and this thing wasn't all that different, it just had more eyes.

I started having the same dream over and over and over: "my crying, no, wailing, had opened some kind of portal on the wall across from my bed, which faced the Space Liquidation Lab, a secret government facility. They advertised how they were able to make space where there was none and none where there was some. The ads didn't make sense to me, but the people in the photos looked really happy. And, when Curt was still here, I wondered if they couldn't make a space for him. Something sound and smell-proof. But I never got around to asking because... life.

So, short of any hard and fast explanation, it just seemed rational, at least in my dream, and then increasingly in real life, that the monsters were coming from the space where Curt might have gone.

It didn't really matter why, because they were here. Not every night, there were nights that were so quiet I'd wake up to the sound of my own crying. But then I'd hear the stomping, smell the stench, and I'd know I wasn't alone.

So, tonight I've chosen to find it comforting. It actually is. Just as long as I ignore him, I'm not alone.

Uncle Otto

When I was twelve my uncle Otto told me I was beautiful. Nobody had ever said that to me before.

Poppa said I was ugly and the reason momma never came home. That was the year she went to Reno to "see relatives." The day she left, Pop said he wasn't feeling well and I would stay with momma's brother, Uncle Otto.

I liked Otto, he smelled nice, like vanilla, and every time he visited he brought me candy and presents. Yet he looked like the burly butcher he was, with a big black beard, strong hands, and belly straining at his shirt.

He picked me up and we took the subway like we had before when momma and pop were yelling. I liked taking the subway and movies with Uncle Otto because he always held my hand, "To make sure you don't get lost." That made me feel safe.

On nights when momma was "feeling poorly," he'd arrive bearing brisket or chicken or liver. Momma took to her bed and he'd cook the best dinners.

But I'd never before been to Uncle Otto's house, a small apartment in the city on Lexington Ave. It was so much nicer than ours, painted a delicious dark purple that made me think of grapes. There were a lot of paintings on the wall of old Greek statues like I'd seen in the Brooklyn Museum.

He sat me on the sofa to watch cartoons while he made dinner. The sofa was green and fuzzy, like grass, and I liked to rub my fingers against it.

Dinner was lamb chops. We never had them at home because momma said they were "too fancy." She said we couldn't afford a "sacrificial lamb." When I asked what that was, she laughed sadly and said, "It's when you sacrifice a lamb to God so that you can get what you want, my little lamb." I liked being called "little lamb." While I didn't know what a sacrifice was, it had to be good if God wanted it.

Uncle Otto's lamb chops, mashed potatoes and peas were the best dinner I ever had. I liked that they were a little sweet, with a peach sauce! Even his dishes were nice, with gold and little flowers around the edge.

Everything Uncle Otto did was pretty and his house was so clean. I felt lucky to have him as my uncle.

After dinner I helped him clean up, which was fun, not like at home where the water was always too hot and the rinse smelled of ammonia. Here we had rubber gloves and the soap smelled like lemon! Uncle Otto and his fruits!

He stood behind me and put his big arms around me, demonstrating the best way to wash a dish by swirling the sponge in circles on the front—and backside, too.

Then we sat together on the sofa and watched "I Love Lucy." We laughed so loud! Uncle Otto had a funny laugh—a high giggle like a girl that only made me laugh even more.

Just like on the subway he held my hand. It was warm and nice but I wondered why since it wasn't like I was going to get lost in his apartment. During the commercial he picked me up, put me on his lap and wrapped his arms around me. He made me feel safe in a way I never did at home.

Momma and pop were always either mad or sad. Nana was just mean. That's what I was used to. But Uncle Otto smiled at me, tousled my hair and made me feel all tingly.

I put my head on his shoulder, his soft curly beard tickling as I sniffed his warm vanilla neck. We sat that way till Lucy cried "Oh, Ricky!" and we laughed again.

He turned off the TV, put sheets and a pillow on the sofa and tucked me in under the softest blanket I'd ever felt.

That's when he kissed me on the forehead, looked me in the eyes and said, "Goodnight my beautiful boy." He turned out the light and went to his bed. I wished he was my pop.

Uncle Otto closed his bedroom door with a click. I tried to stay awake and enjoy the soft couch and the way everything glowed in the moonlight. A few minutes later he was snoring... or crying, I couldn't tell which. I wanted to go hold his hand and make him feel safe... but I fell asleep.

Early next morning Uncle Otto took me home on the subway. At our front steps he gave me a kiss on the forehead and said "I miss you already, beautiful boy."

When I got inside pop was furious. "I saw what you let him do!" I was so surprised I didn't know what to say. Pop stared and said, "Well? What do you have to say for yourself?

"Um, Uncle Otto is nicer..." I stopped before saying "...than you."

"That bitch and her pansy-ass brother! Good riddance to the both of them!"

"I didn't do anything wrong!" I protested.

He yelled, "You let him touch you! You must never let anyone touch you, Aaron!"

I cried, "He's nice!"

"What do you know?"

"He said I'm beautiful."

"You're a freak!" he screamed. Then he touched me the only way he knew how—slapping me so hard I fell on the floor. "You will never see that man again. Or your momma."

He stormed out of the apartment and slammed the door.

I went to bed and cried. I thought of Uncle Otto crying and wished we were together.

Momma never did come back and Pop wasn't home much after that. I wanted to call Uncle Otto but I didn't have his phone number. I looked in the phone book but I didn't know his last name. I took the subway into the city and stopped where I thought we'd gone, but I couldn't find his building.

I was lost with nobody to hold my hand.

Then I had an idea—I would go to the butcher shop where he worked. I remembered the name from the stamp on the meat he brought. Cohen Brothers Kosher Butcher Shop. I looked up the address and left.

There was Uncle Otto—laughing with the ladies who came in. He promised them "the very best, for you, Mrs. Goldfarb, for you, Mrs. Silverberg."

Then, he saw me and his smile disappeared. He turned away and went into the back. There was nothing for me.

I ran down the street, sure there was something terribly wrong with me. Not only could I not be touched, now I couldn't even be looked at.

So I was surprised when Asher, a new boy at school, started talking to me. He'd moved one block over so said we could walk home together. On the way, a bunch of Irish-gang kids started coming up the street towards us.

Asher grabbed my hand and started running. When we finally stopped I looked down and thought, "He must not touch me." But I didn't let go.

He leaned in, brushing the hair out of my eyes, touching my cheek. I didn't die. I felt safe.

I looked into his eyes and I kissed him. Then I pulled away, scared. But he leaned in again and kissed me back, his soft lips tasting like licorice.

We sat there. Our arms around each other's backs, our heads on each other's shoulders.

He said, "you are beautiful." We held hands and he kissed my tears away.

That summer I told him I loved him, and he said he loved me, too. I thought we would be together forever, but his family moved to a Kibbutz and he was gone.

Pop met Ruth, a lady from the temple, and one night she came over to make dinner. Dad gave me a quarter and told me to go to the movies, "Scram, before you scare her away, faygeleh."

I didn't go to the movies. I took the subway into the city, to Cohen's Kosher Butcher Shop. I waited outside for Uncle Otto to leave and quietly followed him—home.

My Right Foot

I lost control of my foot. It just wouldn't do anything. My right foot, my left foot, which foot, I can't tell left from right.

I set it down and it was like standing on a cloud. It felt like it was going through the floor, like that time when I was a kid and there was deep snow and my foot sunk down into it and I couldn't climb up. I was in the backyard freezing and screaming for a half hour before the neighbor finally pulled me out.

I fell over, only this time I was in my living room, not the snow, and there was nobody to pull me out.

So I used my arms to crawl across the floor. The whole time I was thinking, "What's wrong with my foot? I can see it, it's there but it's not working."

I pulled myself up onto a Barcelona chair and I sat there looking at my foot. It didn't look any different. Yet it felt like—nothing.

No, worse than nothing, it felt like it wasn't connected to the rest of my body. No, worse, that it had become some other creature and it wasn't talking to me.

There it was, wearing a wingtip. I wondered what it was thinking. What is this nefarious foot thinking? What was it going to do?

It was attached to my leg, so it couldn't go far... but how was I going to fathom the newly acquired mind of a foot?

My right foot.

I thought perhaps I'd call a doctor, but I couldn't get to my phone because it was over on the table with my keys but now my foot had a mind of its own and wouldn't obey.

I could crawl over, but if I did I wasn't sure I could climb up the slippery chrome table legs —so I started pounding my foot against the floor like when it's asleep—when it's kind of exciting to think, "There's no feeling in my foot now, but it's going to start tingling and hurt!"

Maybe that's what was going on—it didn't have a mind of its own, it was just asleep. I had been sitting on the Mies sofa with my foot curled underneath me...

No, I hadn't! I wouldn't have a shoe on the mohair upholstery, and I most certainly would not be sitting on my shoe while wearing linen pants.

That was the foot talking! The foot was telling some cockamamie story to fool me!

That's one crafty foot!

So I kept banging it against the floor thinking, "I'll show you, fucking foot! I'll show you who's boss. You're attached to me and there's more of me than there is to you!"

But it didn't help. The feeling didn't come back.

I just started hearing pounding from downstairs. Mrs. Schwartz, Stephen's mother, and head of the co-op board. Even in the best of times I had to basically tip toe across my own parquet, now she must have thought I had taken up clog dancing.

Oh, my God, what if my foot takes up clog dancing? Mrs. Schwartz will have me out on my ass.

Why am I even thinking such idiotic things when I have no feeling in my foot?

It's putting thoughts in my head, that's what it's doing. Not just thinking, now, now it's making me see things. I see a rabbit on the piano. A real, live fuzzy white rabbit with Sinatra blue eyes on the Steinway.

That's not good. It's not good for the lacquer, it's going to scratch the finish. What if it pees on the keys? That's a fine way to treat a Steinway.

But I'm not sure it's really there, maybe the foot is just making me think it's there, then I hear myself thinking this, thinking that the foot is telling me what to think and I think I'm crazy.

No, I know I'm crazy because other people's feet don't generally do this.

Except my right foot has always been very shrewd. When they say to put your best foot forward they're talking about my right foot. Whenever I'm doing a deal, I get this feeling in my toe and if it's cramping I know it's a bad idea and I've always listened to my toe.

The podiatrist told me it was arthritis and I thought, "I don't give a fuck what it is, my toe has never failed me!"

I don't know if this is the toe talking or if it's me, but I'm taken back to all those Bugs Bunny cartoons and all I can hear is, "Kill the Wabbit," which really doesn't make sense because the Kashmiri silk carpet is white and I would never get the blood out.

I must be pretty high.

I took LSD gummy bears for my bad back and my dealer said they were mild but maybe I shouldn't have had a handful.

Oooh, the little dots in my wingtip, the brogue holes, they're moving around. They made a face!

My foot's going to make a pronouncement!

"You are not high," my foot just said, "I am in control."

OK, well, there shoots the high theory, the foot is in control. Well, I don't know, maybe this is not such a bad thing, maybe, at last, I can cede control of my life over to my foot because it knows best anyway.

I can finally stop worrying about everything all the time, worried about currency trajectories, worried about futures, worried about puddles.

I'll put that best foot forward and follow it and won't have to worry about anything— ever!

Now the little dots on the brogue are smiling! Yes, yes, this is the right thing to do! My toe is tapping!

Maybe my foot will get me tap lessons. I always wanted to do that when I was a kid. My dad said that wasn't a manly thing to do and I had to play football instead.

Maybe now my dream will come true and I can become a tap dancer. Wear one of those sparkly suits. I'll be known as the "fleet feet of Wall Street!"

This could be a whole new career for me! I don't think I'd have any competition in that vertical market.

This is FANTASTIC! I LOVE THIS!

Uh oh, wait a second, I'm getting a cramp, a cramp in my left foot. What's happening? Is the left foot jealous? It should be, my left foot is nothing compared to my right. It never tells me anything. It's the one that slipped on ice three years ago in Paris sent me to the emergency room when I was supposed to meet with Marie on top of the Eiffel Tower and I never did and she took it personally and I never saw her again.

I lost what could have been the love of my life because of this fucking left foot! "Cut it off, cut it off!" my right foot just told me—it has a plan!

I must go to the kitchen but I'm not sure if I can stand up. I'll stop trying and just let my right foot be in control... It's standing, it's balancing—that right foot is something else!

Now the left foot, nope, nope, twisted, falling, head narrowly missing the edge of the marble coffee table. That can kill a person.

My left foot was trying to kill me! Fucking left foot!

Now it's kicked off its shoe, sent it flying, oh, no! Sent it right into an important Lalique Chrysanthemum vase! A $60,000 vase in shards, sparkling on the floor, that's very pretty. But, no, not cool, fucking left foot I hate you!

Right foot, you're not going to take that lying down are you? No, no, the right foot is kicking the left foot—kick it, KICK IT! Kick that motherfucking foot! KICK THE SHIT OUT OF IT!

Ow, that hurts, it hurts. It doesn't hurt my right foot because I can't feel it but it does hurt my left—but it's necessary! Necessary because the left foot has been bad, very bad, it must be punished!

God, I wish I could do this to other people! I wish I could kick the crap out of people with my right foot, that would be so fucking great!

Oooh, ooh, my right foot wants to play the piano! I always wanted to play the piano. That would be great. The decorator picked that piano. I always thought I might take a lesson but I never had the time or interest.

Now it's time, but how can I get over there, my left foot is in terrible, terrible pain. Right foot to the rescue—look, it has an almost prehensile ability now to drag me as if I was a monkey, it's amazing!

I pull myself up, hoist my right foot to the piano. It's Rhapsody in Blue! I'm playing Gershwin with my right foot!

What dexterity! What a sense of rhythm! What panache!

Wait—wait! It's calling on my left foot to be reasonable, and now, as I lean back and grasp the back of the piano bench I can lift my left foot.

My right foot is playing Rhapsody in Blue while the left plays American in Paris! It's a medley, they fit perfectly together, I had no idea that the music did this! Bernstein never noticed—but my right foot did!

This is, perhaps, the most beautiful music I have ever heard in my entire life!

If only I had my phone I could be recording this, put it on YouTube and become a sensation. I could make millions from advertising affiliate fees and become a master of new media overnight.

Dammit.

Well, if my right foot can do this now, it can do it again later, so I'm going to relax and listen to this music, let it wash over me.

I don't think I've ever had a better time in my entire life.

I LOVE MY RIGHT FOOT! I FUCKING LOVE IT!

Papa needs a new pair of shoes—no, the foot is telling me it never wants to wear shoes again! This may limit my mobility during the winter months but so be it!

Now the music is finished and—we're off! Both feet clawing at the carpet, pulling my limp upper body behind it. My upper body seems to have no control at all, my arms trailing behind my head, my head dragging on the carpet, which, luckily is 100% silk and not creating static. I hate static in my hair.

I'm not sure where we're going—oh, to my briefcase! Now, wow, my feet are, I don't know how they, how they, how they entered the briefcase password without being able to see it, but they did it entirely by feel! They opened it!

And now both feet are holding pens. My hands, my lazy hands, they're only right handed, but look, the right foot is instructing the left foot and they are both drawing now.

I can't see what from this position and I can't raise my head. I can only imagine what they're drawing. I'll try very hard to lift my neck and see, it looks, it looks like, it looks like a self-portrait of my feet in the style of MC Escher. Brilliant!

My feet are geniuses now, both of them. I don't hate the left one any longer now that it's in cahoots with the right.

I LOVE my feet. I'm so glad I've been getting pedicures all this time otherwise they might be angry with me.

Now my right foot is holding up the drawing, no, it's not of my feet—it's the Mona Lisa's! Nobody has ever seen her feet, not even DaVinci—I am the first!

This is a miraculous revelation! This will take the art world by storm!

But wait, wait—the feet are folding it now, in an origami, no, wait a second, it's a paper plane, but not just a normal one, no, it's an B-2 Stealth bomber!

My right foot is launching it, launching it through the 55th floor window, out towards Central Park—of course, of course! Towards the Metropolitan Museum where one of the curators is sure to find it and hail my feet as New Masters, the greatest artists of the 21st century!

Now my feet are pulling me, pulling me, pulling me, dragging me behind them, towards the front door.

I wonder where we're going!

We're going down the hallway, down the hallway, oh, hello Mrs. Schwartz! I'm unable to move my hands to wave—oh, my foot has waved—no! It has smacked her upside the head in a swift Karate move and now my feet continue to drag me down the hallway.

I have surrendered my entire life to my feet, and they are taking me down the concrete fire stairs.

Oh, oh my head! Oh my head! Oh my head! Oh my head! Oh my head! Oh my head!

I hope we're not going down 55 flights of stairs—but if we are I'm sure they have a good reason.

I have a headache now, and I'm rather sleepy.

And I just noticed I'm not wearing anything but sock garters!

The feeling is returning to my right foot, where there's a great deal of pain. As in my head.

I'm starting to wonder if I'll end up on Page 6 with a headline that says, "Bond King Found Nearly Naked In Stairwell."

I still can't move my arms.

This concrete is cold on my ass.

Fucking-A! This is even better than last Saturday!

Batter

Everything went red like I'd been hit in the head with the setting sun. Just blurry outlines and red. Everything I knew retreated, hid somewhere in the back of my brain where it no longer mattered.

All I wanted to do was lash out. Lash out at the thing that made me feel this way. This horrible, alien creature in the kitchen, wielding a knife. Sickening. My arms tingled. My head was pressurized to the point of explosion.

There was only one way to end it. I picked up the chair and smashed it down on the monster—over and over again till it stopped threatening, stopped moving. The knife in its hand was released, lying on the linoleum in a growing pool of something on the floor.

My legs were shaking and I could no longer stand—I landed on my tailbone, on the floor, in the wetness. I sat there, feeling my head deflate and trying to find oxygen in the room. My hands were wet with whatever was on the floor.

Color started returning, like a Polaroid picture developing. The monster on the floor became mottled white and pink covered in an apron of tiny yellow flowers. I followed the flabby, flaccid arm to its end and the knife had somehow turned into a spatula. The spatula whose patterns matched those on my arms and legs.

The liquid on the floor was pancake batter with streaks of red working their way through like hellish rivers.

The memories and thoughts crawled from the back of my head to the front and I recognized the figure on the floor. It was my mother. Her eyes wide open, staring blankly at me.

I smelled something burning and the smoke started billowing from the pan on the stove. I tried to get up and slipped in the bloody batter and landed with my face close to hers. That face she used to push close to mine while she was screaming. Only now, she was silent. I was silent. No crying, no begging, "please stop, mom, please stop, mom!"

She had stopped.

For once, her face didn't look angry or disappointed. She just looked like a sad, ugly old woman. If she had been anyone else I would have felt sorry for her. But I couldn't.

I slipped again and almost fell on top of her. I grabbed the table, pulled myself up and turned off the gas under the burning pan. I put the pan in the sink and filled it with water that spattered, grease hitting me, hitting me, hitting. For the last time.

My Sainted Old Man

This is bullshit. I turned 21 two weeks ago. I should be able to buy beer. Fucking old man at the cash register and his fucking old man rules.

I didn't know I couldn't buy beer because Brad's under 21. What kind of crap is that? I could have just left him in the car. What the fuck difference does it make.

I've been drinking beer with my Dad since I was 12. We used to get bombed together. That was before he ran his F-150 into a tree, but drinking didn't have anything to do with it, he could hold his own. It was one of those assholes he always talked about, at CalTrans, fucked with his brakes or something to kill him before he could get 'em fired. He always said he was gonna get 'em fired.

The world is fucked. I've known that since I was 12, too. Dad was a super cool guy, always good to me, shared his beer and his weed with me. Didn't have to go sit next to a dumpster behind Safeway to get stoned like Brad did. His father was a prick—didn't let him do anything. Then his father got busted for watching kiddie porn or something. Taxes, maybe, I don't know, but I always thought he was creepy. What kind of dad won't get high with his only son? That's just pushing the kid out the door so he'll do worse, which is what Brad did.

I only tried crack once, with Brad, I didn't like it. My dad didn't either, he said if I was going to try it he was gonna be there with me, and we all did it, and Brad was used to it but it made me sick—I thought there were purple monsters with two mouths coming out of Brad's butt. Yeah, laugh at it now but it was a fucking nightmare. Dad was there for me, slapping me out of it and passing out on the floor by my bed after I went to sleep.

And it was Dad who got Brad into rehab and off that shit. Not his worthless do-gooder dad, working for some charity supposedly, driving his fucking Prius and not eating meat or wearing leather. Why didn't that fucker drive into a tree?

My dad was practically a saint, even Brad says so. Always had my back. Fucking bureaucracy wanted to say he was drunk driving but there wasn't no beer in the car and his blood alcohol was below the limit so they had to pay his life insurance.

Brad lives with me now. His dad had a fit, but couldn't stop him when he turned 18. We're just bros, not nothing else. I gotta girlfriend, Ciel, cool chick I met at Dad's funeral. She

246 - Daniel Will-Harris

does makeup on the dead people, and she covered up all of Dad's bruises and made him look good. I hope I look as good as he did when I get old and die.

Brad's had a hard life so I take care of him like my Dad did for me. His mom left with some other guy when he was just a kid— what kind of cunt does that? I don't call her that when he's around, it'd hurt him, but come on, motherfucker. I'm sure it was 'cause of his dad being such a prick—and probably into weird shit in bed. Brad tells this story about hearing "mooing" from his folks' bedroom when he was only 5, we both laugh our asses off about it. A course, they lived next door to a dairy, so it could have been that, but I can imagine his fucking vegan father playing the bull. Gross. But funny.

So alls I'm trying to do is get Brad a little buzz for his birthday. He's turning 19 in a couple of weeks and birthdays are always a hard time. My dad'd give me a baggie for my birthday, you know, shit I could use. His dad gave him —OK, you aren't gonna believe this—his dad gave him little "certificates" saying that he'd donated money to charity. Who does that to a kid? That's hateful. My dad would always have a little something for Brad, some weed, one or two of those tiny liquor bottles you get on airplanes, useful fun shit.

And we'd all get high together and watch porn—guy stuff.

But the old fucker at the register won't let me buy booze. Fine, I drop Brad off at home and come back by myself. Old fart's not at the register so I tell the girl who's there that he wouldn't let me and I've come back by myself. What the fuck—she's calling the manager and it's the old fart. Fucking hell.

Oh, fuck you all, you haters, you losers, working at some crappy store at 11 at night when you should be home drinking or fucking. Fuck you.

I screamed all the way out to the car and burned some rubber out of the parking lot. Can't do that in a fucking Prius. Fine, I'll go to Safeway—it's 10 minutes away but there's nothing I wouldn't do for Brad. Like there was nothing my dad wouldn't do for me.

God, I miss him.

Push Pull

The door said pull. I pushed. Oh, great start, Gail. That'll make a good impression. They'll think you're either illiterate or uncoordinated. Maybe both.

I'll just find my keys and go home now. Where did I put them?

But before I can find them, a beautiful young woman is opening the door from the inside.

"Oh, don't mind that, I do that all the time," she says kindly, not at all patronizing as I would have done at her age.

I was young and beautiful, too. Now...

Why am I here? I hadn't planned on coming here today. I mean, I'm wearing yoga clothes, but I didn't think I'd actually stop here.

There's a lovely little French bakery, Brioche Bleu, next door—I thought I'd get a cappuccino and a Meyer lemon croissant. No, that's what I had with Maddie...

I was having lunch with Maddie, who's been a real friend to me through everything, the accident and break... She looked especially good. Not thin, that's not Maddie—but happy, smiling, normally pretty rare for her— reserved for that short time between when you order a chocolate croissant and it actually arrives.

Now she was smiling even after we'd finished our croissants.

I asked her what she was on, because I was going to pull one of those "ask your doctor is SmiloLift if right for you" things—I'd take anything.

When she said "Pilates" at first I just heard "pill" and almost burned my tongue on the espresso.

Maddie wasn't a physical person like I was— she was smart. I know it's possible to be both but I'm not. I was pretty and athletic and so I had three career avenues open to me, I could be a girl's gym teacher (OK), a lady golfer (boring), or a prostitute (creepy). That third choice wasn't on the APTitest I took in 11th grade, it was just something that career counselor, Mr. Lear, seemed to imply until I kicked him in the balls.

So, Gym Coach it was, with all that implied. But, look, when you're a woman, teaching a bunch of girls, who are you going to meet but women? Yeah, there are the male coaches but they're usually assholes or in the closet. My friends tried to fix me up with smart guys but I found them too boring and they found me too... tall.

So I focused on work—started the first Girl's LaCrosse league, got our basketball team into nationals and co-coached the swim team with Tally Rand, our Finnish exchange teacher and my best...

"I didn't know you were a friend of Madeline's..." the beautiful young woman says—Oh, yes, exercise place... She looks like Snow White—pale skin, dark hair, gorgeous girl, big smile, but not too big like Mary Tyler Moore or Julia Roberts.

"Yes, very good friend." I manage to say while wondering if my hair was ever that thick or shiny.

"She's doing so much better!" she says, helping me off with my jacket, even though I didn't ask and... she smells like pine and pepper. "I know you've been through a lot, we'll help you feel better," she says, smiling, with that teeth and those hair...

I wonder how she knows... Maddie must have told her, of course...

"I'm so honored you came to me—I hope I can help you the way you helped me," smile.

How did I help her? She looks familiar... her top says "Janine" and I'm thinking, "Her name's not Janine..."

"Janey?" I say, "Janey Browne?"

"It's Browne-Gold now, my married name, and I go by Janine, but you can still call me Janey."

Oh my God, it's little Janey. Runt of the class. Couldn't do a pull up to save her life, with those tooth-picky arms. Always tripping over her own feet. She wasn't good at anything.

"I wasn't good at anything until you suggested swimming!" she lit up that smile again and I smiled, a reflex, like a doctor's little red rubber hammer against my cheek.

"You changed my life." she says—and I remember, I remember it all, down to washing off the chlorine in the shower and

Tally's "Gee Your Hair Smells Terrific" shampoo.

It was 20 years and maybe 2,000 girls ago, but a girl stands out when she wins an Olympic medal, even a Bronze one.

She's talking but I am back, 20 years, remembering the little girl who couldn't do anything. All that time in the pool with Tally...

Then I hear her say, "...if there had been acceptance speeches at the Olympics I would have thanked you!"

"That's so nice—but I just started you out— you had the talent and the drive, you were always in the pool before everyone else and back at night, I remember."

And I can remember it all so clearly. I don't know why that is. 20 years ago like yesterday and yesterday I can't remember at all. They said it would be like this but it doesn't make any sense and it makes me mad.

"I'll walk you through it all—nothing to remember—and I'll make a video with my iPhone so you can watch it." she says, being so nice, so very nice, like the nurses, like...

"Thank you, Janey, you're being very nice, I just stopped by to get a croissant."

"They're next store—we can both get one after the session."

Oh, that's right. The session. The sun is streaming through the window and the words on the window are making a shadow on the floor that says "setalip xallarap." I don't like it when words do that, it happens sometimes when I'm trying to read the newspaper, too. Oh, it's OK in the window, "Parallax Pilates."

So I lie on this thing that looks like a cross between a treadmill and a bondage bench and she puts my feet in straps and I lift myself—it's easy and it feels good.

I always wished I could fly. After hours, Tally and I would dive off the high-board and that was like flying. We started doing synchronized dives and that's when I fell in love with her—flying off the high-dive, looking in her eyes for a split second before the twisting double-somersault.

24 years. We lived in condos next to each other. We were "best friends." Then she...

"Are you OK, Gail?"

Oh—I'm here, in this place with Janey.

"You're doing great—but let's not push it, OK?" she says as she helps me down to the bench.

Those teeth. That hair. The sun behind her, making her glow like...

"I'm OK, Tally."

"Janey,"

"Sorry, I was just thinking..."

"I know. You both inspired me."

"She moved back to Finland," I say. Hearing the words reminds me it's real. "While I was in the coma. Nobody thought I'd wake up."

The pretty girl isn't smiling. I wish she was. She looks like Tally when she smiles.

I see her turning away and wiping her eyes.

"Maybe you'd like to come to my house for dinner. Denise would love to meet you."

I am trying to remember how to get home. My house is yellow.

She says "I'd love for you to meet my wife."

Little dust specs are floating in the air, like divers who never have to land.

She who can create the Truth

I t has finally cooled down—Thank the Empress! It is a sweet sign to see the thermometer in single digits, only 97 degrees. I can't remember the last time it was under a hundred. And now, Praise the Empress. She has done it and she said she would.

She said she would speak to the sun and tell it that her land must be cooler and she has accomplished that as we all knew that she would as she is capable of anything which is why we pledge our eternal loyalty to Her.

Like her great great grandfather before, she is from a line of strong leaders, with a holy microphone from Her mouth to God's ear.

What she says is truth, so, so much better for this land than it used to be when mere mortals had to make our own decisions. Why? Why would anyone want to do that when your majestic leader can simply decree the truth?

The truth this morning is that it is cooler and the truth tomorrow is that it may not be and that is just the truth and how happy we are to be able to know the truth so we may live the truth.

If the truth is that it is 120 degrees because The Empress has decreed that we must sweat to purify our bodies, then it is 120 degrees and we purify our bodies. Praise the Empress.

If She decrees we must not eat for three days because we need to purify our spirits then we do not eat for three days and we rejoice in her majesty and her truth telling—in her truth creation.

Because who is more powerful than she who can create the truth?

I uncovered old photographs from my ancestors, living in those dark ages of democracy. We have been taught to see the fear under their smiles as they stand beside the horrible houses they were forced to buy and live indoors. And their dangerous and wrongly colorful automobiles they needed to move from place to place—too far, too fast.

Now we know the benefits of staying in our proper place, and walking only as far as we are told by Our Betters who we carry on our backs.

We know how good this is for us because the Empress has told us. So I feel pride even when it is 120 degrees!

Today She declared the truth that I do not need as much water as the Better on my back! I feel pride in carrying him and grateful for giving what I can to the greater good because we are all working for this greater good!

How wonderful to know she has made our world for us! We were taught as children about the horrible past, vile and disgusting, where people were only out for themselves. This is a concept now so hard to fathom. Look at this tent I live in, this is not my tent, it is our tent and I'm grateful to be able to shield myself from the sun in this tent.

And when I carry Betters back to the palaces, they are not their palaces, they are ours. We all own them together. We share in the wealth of this great empire and the Betters live there because of the hard work they do on our behalf.

They have sacrificed themselves and their lives and their families to work tirelessly—for us! They are doing the greater work. So they must endure the guilt and shame of living apart from the people, and we all know how shameful that is.

I remember in school seeing a picture of a tent and underneath it "for good," in bright yellow, then there was a picture of a palace and under it the black words "for shame."

They suffer for our good and so I am honored when they are on my back knowing their sacrifice for me, having to endure living indoors in those frigid places. I carried one in and it was so cold I did not know how they could bear it, not knowing the beauty of the hot open air as we all do.

Our Betters are forced to live like those stupid, disgusting heathens from the past rather than in the way that Empress intended. They must envy me, close to the land, close to each other, millions of us as far as the eye can see in this camp.

We are given water and we are given food—
when the Empress decrees we should have it.
We are given it. Unlike in the past where
people had to buy it. I am grateful for all I am
given.

I am grateful for the choke collar I wear that
shocks to remind me I need to work for the
greater good, so grateful because human
nature is slothful and greedy and our collars
are sacred reminders of the Empress' love for
us—that she cares enough to give us these
beautiful shiny black collars so we can feel
her loving touch.

Ouch. For Emperess' sake! I must go and pick
up a Better and carry them to the official
white palace! Oh, the great honor of this!
Perhaps just perhaps I will catch a glimpse,
even a shadow of her majesty, Empress
Ivanka IV.

Walking from comfort

I walk—step by step—away from those I love—from things that bring me pleasure. Treading, from the known.

I am walking north, into the mountains, away from the embracing heat, into what I have heard is stabbing cold.

It is where I need to be. Anywhere but here.

I was born a fortunate one, to a father, mother and family that had been in Kashmir for generations. We were settled with roots as deep as a Chinar tree.

Everything needed to sustain us flowing from the earth like water, making lives as sweet as sap.

Silken robes in colors like flowers, soft carpets beneath our feet. Soft of hand, fair as the moon. And I, promised to Ghazala, would start our family and take my place in the apogee of leaders.

And yet, the trees did not bend to my will. As I was riding my horse through the Chinar, I was hit by a branch and knocked to the ground.

My leg was broken. I could not so much as stand. There I lay as day turned to night, then night to day. I was forced to see that the comfort in my daily life did not come from me, that I merely partook in it as a hummingbird to nectar.

There I was—helpless—worse, useless—worse, hopeless. Crying under a Chinar.

It was then, when I feared I might never return home, that I saw a small old peasant. He was dressed in rags, and smelled like an animal. He had no shoes, and his eyes were cloudy, yet he had found my horse at the river and followed him here.

And while in my daily life, this was not a man I would have even glanced at, now, anyone with two legs who could walk was like a god.

Though frail and old, leathered by the sun, he hoisted me onto my horse and I rode while he walked towards my palace.

I had been riding too proudly, too fast, so I did not see the branch that took me down. Now, at this slow walking pace, it took all day to return.

Occasionally he would stop to water the horse, and me, holding the water in his filthy hands, to my lips. And I drank, gratefully, as my thirst was greater than my fear.

When he spoke, it was in the most gentle tone, making me feel as if this man was my savior, lest I die broken and alone at only 28.

I told him when he returned me I would gift him with gold and gemstones, necklaces and rings, and he would be a wealthy man.

He thanked me for my generosity, but said he imagined it did not mean very much to me as I had so much I would not miss it.

I thought about his words in the slow rhythm of the horses hooves and the light step of his feet. He said he did not require wealth, that when I gave him those things he would give them to the poor—that an entire village might live a lifetime from the value of one ruby ring.

This made my heart ache more than my leg. I did not know this. I had never cared to know. I had never seen these people, or for one single moment thought past the beauty of the ring itself to the value it might have to them.

He told me he had come from a fine family in the north. He had everything he wanted, but nothing he needed.

And, again, my heart felt tired and the world looked hard. The towns that had been a beautiful blur as I galloped by were littered with sadness. So many trees cut, he told me, for fire and warmth. Mounds of dead flowers along the side of the road where infants were buried.

I had never seen these things yet they were always right beneath my gaze.

Finally, it occurred to me to ask of this man, why was he on this path, this path to finding me.

For the first time he smiled, and he said, "Thank you for asking about me."

I realized that as far as I could remember, I had not asked, much less cared, about others, what they were doing or feeling. I could become so obsessed with a pebble in my sandal that I did not even see our servants toiling, carrying rocks.

It had been in my eyes all this time, but only now could I see it.

He told me of himself, and how one day while hunting stags he was accidentally shot with an arrow. When it pierced his thigh, he felt for the first time the pain of the animals he had hunted all his life.

His brother, who had shot him, removed the arrow and helped him limp home.

The pain of every step opened his eyes—and heart—to the world around him, as mine were now being opened. By the time he reached his palatial family home, it no longer felt like his. Just as he now felt that nothing belonged to anyone.

Much to the chagrin of his family and intended, he left on a quest, he told them. "For riches" he said, to satisfy them. Yet he knew the riches he sought were waiting to be uncovered somewhere in his heart.

That was 40 years ago and he had spent every day since walking, asking others about themselves. The way I had, for the first time, asked about him.

There I was, on that horse, unable to walk, while this man who had given up everything was leading me on foot. Now all I wanted to do was follow him.

As we reached the gates of the palace, he said, "This is where I leave you." Tears in my eyes, I told him of my gratitude to him for opening my heart. For saving my life, spiritually, as well as physically.

I took off my necklace and my rings and handed them to him and said, "Use them as you will in the good of others. But please, please come back when my leg is healed so that I may follow you."

He smiled, kindly, held my hand as he lowered me from the horse, and said, "You have no need to follow me, I am nearing the end of my path and you are just starting on yours."

I said, "But how will I find my way?"

He said to me, "The same way that I did. By knowing that the way—is no way."

He kissed my cheek and I saw one of my tears glisten on his lips.

He brought out my sadness like a waterfall, and took it on, like a river.

I watched him disappear into the Chinar trees, knowing I would never see him again and realizing I had neglected to ask his name.

Daniel
Will-Harris

Daniel Will-Harris is a best-selling author of five novels and stage plays.

MoMA has called Daniel's work "truly unique."

His 9 books have sold over 300,000 copies. He has three produced feature film screenplays to his credit and has written over 600 short stories currently featured in his popular story podcast. He's also an award-winning designer of wristwatches.

He's developed plays with the Kennedy Center Playwriting Intensive, Naked Angels Theater, and The Actor's Centre in London.

To learn his "Write in the Now" writing practice, go to www.WriteInTheNow.com

You can see all his work and contact him here: www.will-harris.com